Eyehill

Eyehill

KELLY COOPER

Edited by Laurel Boone.
Cover illustration "Calmer Willow," © Robert Pohl, 1996.
Cover and book design by Julie Scriver.
Printed in Canada by Transcontinental.
10 9 8 7 6 5 4 3 2 1

National Library of Canada Cataloguing in Publication

Cooper, Kelly, 1963-
Eyehill / Kelly Cooper.

ISBN 0-86492-379-1

1. Saskatchewan — Fiction.   I. Title.
PS8555.O59215E94 2004   C813'.6   C2004-900161-2

Published with the financial support of the Canada Council
for the Arts, the Government of Canada through the Book
Publishing Industry Development Program, and the
New Brunswick Culture and Sports Secretariat.

Goose Lane Editions
469 King Street
Fredericton, New Brunswick
CANADA E3B 1E5
www.gooselane.com

To the people of Senlac,
Jim and Sharon Cooper in particular

Contents

N. Loves Peggy

A few hours after Jarvis was conceived, his father's body began to swell. McGowan's skin erupted, hive upon hive, his joints locked into position, and his brain ballooned against the confines of his skull. Earlier in the week, he'd caught the drift from a spray plane. The doctor offered no explanation and no cure beyond a painkiller, so McGowan's wife painted him with calamine lotion and applied cool cloths to the soles of his burning feet.

After five days, he was able to get out of bed and wash his face. He stood before the bathroom sink, almost too weak to work up a lather on the soap with his shaving brush. He dabbed his chin, seeing himself reflected, thinner and whiter, but otherwise the same man. He lifted the razor, unaware of the cells which made up his whiskers, the cells of the skin of his face, the cells of the blood and the jawbone, still ignorant of that one cell, the single sperm that was, at the very moment of his looking in the mirror, merged with the egg of his wife and dividing. The DNA of those cells now had a mutation, a change that might show itself, if it were visible, as a hook or a blossom or a gap.

Jarvis would be born in the ice storm of 1970, his head crowning as the freezing rain glazed the windows of the Airedale Hospital and snapped the limbs off the Manitoba maples and the black poplars that sheltered the building from the wind. Newspapers called the storm a freak of nature, and as time passed, Jarvis himself was sometimes called the same. One day he climbed the tallest tree in the schoolyard, too high (as usual), too fast (as usual), and he slipped, impaling himself on the sharp end of a broken branch. The wood tore his pants and cut him just below the groin, but he made it to the ground himself, clutching the blood-stained crotch of his jeans. Later, when the wound was almost healed, he bragged of his luck to the schoolyard audience.

"Just glad that branch missed my package. A target that big . . ."

"My father says God has his reasons," Roland Lafonde said. "Who knows what great plans the Almighty has for your dink?"

"Show us your scar," another boy said. "I don't believe the branch came that close."

Most of us, with the exception of the Federal Grain agent's son, grew up on farms south of Eyehill, a town of about a hundred and twenty with no bank, no hospital, no high school. Jarvis and I shared a sense of destiny, not much else, and even that showed itself differently. The McGowans were steady, methodical men who took apart motors and laid all the parts in order on the pages of old newspaper saved for that purpose. But Jarvis? He was a high-wire act. We all knew that someday he would do something both foolhardy and heroic.

"You want to stay here all your life?" he'd demand.

"No."

"Well?"

I said nothing, developed patterns of silence, knowing my refusal to answer drove him craziest of all.

He is hidden somewhere in the dark between the train tracks and the Wheat Pool elevator's high wall, waiting for his chance to jump out of the shadows and say, Gotcha. He knows boxcars scare me, especially boxcars after dark, but he's hiding anyway because he is that kind of boy.

Roxanna's brother found a hobo's nest once, on the front of a boxcar. Not in the car, but outside in the little fenced-in part up front where the cars join one to the other. He found a blanket, a tube of toothpaste and a half-empty jar of peanut butter.

"Jarvis?" I whisper.

I'm afraid to straddle one of the couplings and cross to the other side, because the movement will put me directly in front of the little fenced-in part, and there might be a hobo there, a man with a rag soaked in chloroform who will clamp the rag (a wad of dirty handkerchief) over my mouth, and my last memory will be of my own voice, calling for Jarvis.

A hand reaches out from under the car and grabs me by the ankle.

I suck in a lungful of air, try to scream, but what comes out of me is a long gasp. I lift my free foot and slam the full weight of my snow boot down on the wrist attached to the hand that traps me. If it belongs to a stranger, I'm for sure going to get away. If it belongs to Jarvis, well, he's got it coming.

Jarvis grunts.

I drop down on my knees to look under the car. He's lying on his back. A tray of little paint pots, the kind that comes with model cars and airplanes, rests on his chest, and he holds a brush in the other hand.

We are supposed to be at the Community Hall, serving strawberry shortcake as a fundraiser for the 4-H Club. So far, everything is going as we planned. He left first, slipping out the door that led from the kitchen. I followed a few minutes later. The railroad track is only a three minute jog from the hall.

"My hands are freezing," he says. He brings the brush up to his chest, slants it into the paint and dabs at the metal under-belly, the movements awkward in the cramped space.

"Can you see?"

"Not much. Your turn."

Slide my back over the steel rail onto the wooden ties in the center of the track. Jarvis scrunches over and out the other side, leaving me the paint and the brush. On the crossbar above I see J.M., his initials, wobbly but legible. My turn. I put some paint on the brush and make a mark on the crossbar. Nothing shows up. Must be a dark colour, black, maybe, or navy blue, but I can't lift my head high enough to see what colours are in the tray. I try again, dipping into another pot, dragging the brush across the steel to make the shape of the letter R.

"Hurry up," Jarvis says. The lights of a car flash by.

I put the R for Rhea right above the J. My last name is Jardine. I paint over his J with my brush, so now our initials are linked, mine running vertically, his horizontally. By the time I finish outlining the curve of his J, he's gone (of course), but I know he'll be waiting for me somewhere, concealed in one of the shadowed spaces between the railway track and the hall. I lie on my back for a few more breaths, imagining the train moving, our two names hurtling toward the Pacific Ocean; ten years later, waiting for a different train to pass at a highway crossing, I'll see graffiti sprayed on the sides of the cars and think, if it weren't for Carmela, Jarvis might have left Eyehill with me.

Reading on the school bus makes me feel sick, but I do it anyway because the book gives me a reason to ignore Jarvis. After grade nine, Eyehill sends its children twenty-five miles away, to the larger school in Airedale. What Say Warzecka drives the bus, his rear-view mirror adjusted so he can keep an eye on the seats at the back. Most of the time, he doesn't use the mirror anyway. He just drives, both hands on the wheel, arms straight on either side. He often drives right by roads where he is supposed to turn. When things got bad and he couldn't make a go of it farming, he rented his land and began this new career, but not before years of field work done on a cabless tractor pretty much deafened him.

During the last fifteen minutes of the route, Jarvis and I are the only ones left on the bus, and this is when Jarvis wants to have conversations. Not when we're at school, because he's a year older, for one thing, part of a large, intimidating group of boys who line up with their backs against the hallway walls, judging the girls unlucky enough or bold enough to walk that gauntlet. For another, I'm no use to him.

Jarvis has become the king of one-night stands and, as well, an obvious social climber. At parties, he picks up easy girls and takes them outside for an hour or so, but he never asks them on a date. The girls he does ask out are the popular ones: pretty girls, girls on the volleyball team, exotic girls from foreign countries visiting Airedale on exchange programs. When one of them says yes, then he really thinks he's done something: Jarvis from a hick town like Eyehill getting a date with a girl at the top of the ladder. It's all sex and status with him. Right now, he's supposed to be dating Carmela. She's a local girl, so I don't suppose it will last long, but she's pretty and popular, even with the guys from Airedale. Before he asked her out, she'd call me on the phone and say, "How can you stand to just be friends with him?"

I was always the only girl invited to Jarvis's birthday parties. We just are.

"Good book?" he asks.

The book giving me motion sickness today is *The Edible Woman*, at least that's what the dust jacket says. What I am, in fact, reading is *Riders of the Purple Sage*, my all-time favourite Zane Grey western. The Atwood cover is to fool Ms. Sloan, who thinks I have a special interest in Atwood because I chose her as the subject for my Biography of a Canadian Writer assignment. Turns out Ms. Sloan went to school with Margaret Atwood. We called her Peggy, she said. No one suspected what she would become.

I nod. Yes, it's a good book. Lassiter has just ridden into town on a blind horse, and things don't look good for the Mormons.

"I thought from the title it might be a dirty book. Any good parts like that?"

"It's not dirty. It's literature." I stop reading long enough to tell him the story of Ms. Sloan and Margaret Atwood and how she was just Peggy.

"Neil Young sings a song about a girl called Peggy."

"Who's Neil Young?"

Jarvis hangs out with a bunch of older guys at Denis Lafonde's trailer. They sit around listening to music from the sixties.

"You don't know Neil Young? You couldn't be more out of it."

I ignore him, knowing he wants a reaction. The bus bounces over ruts. The lines of print on the page move up and down like a printout from one of those lie detectors on the cop shows. It seems the conversation is over until he asks, "How old's this Atwood?"

"Forty-seven."

"She's older than he is. Some guys like older women. Where's she from?"

"Ontario." *She came to know intimately the bush country of Northern Ontario*, my research said.

"See. I knew it. Some of Neil Young's first gigs were in Northern Ontario. I bet they had a thing going." He starts singing, *"Don't call pretty Peggy, she can't hear you no more."* He hums for a another mile or two before saying, "She left him, probably. Broke his heart. Typical woman."

I keep my eyes on the book. I know he's staring, but I won't look back. I tell myself it's just Jarvis, the boy who persuaded me to ride my bicycle down the Johnson Hill with my feet off the pedals, who ran for help when the front tire hit a rock and the handlebars spun out of my hands, who threw up when he found an adult because he'd been running so hard and because he thought I was dead (my nose was broken and there was a lot of blood).

Just Jarvis.

My skin doesn't feel the brush of every thread in the weave of my shirt. I don't care about how, without even looking at him, I know his hand is only two inches away from my shoulder.

"You'll never get anywhere," he says. "You've got no imagination."

Not long after that, Jarvis starts working for my father. The spring's been wet and cold; there are a lot of calves with pneumonia. The sickest ones are easy to catch, but the ones that have already had a shot or two of antibiotic have to be chased and cornered in the corral. I run after a little black one with a white face, grab its hind leg and pull. The calf hops backward on three legs until Jarvis throws it on its side, pinning it to the ground and holding the legs immobile while I slide the needle into the soft fold of skin where the animal's neck meets its shoulder.

A cow comes to the feed trough with bloody shreds of placenta hanging from under her tail but no calf. We're sent out on foot to search the pasture closest to the house. Probably dead, my father says, but we'd better look. I hate the thought of finding it, stretched out on a hilltop maybe, where it's warm enough for crocuses and everything with leaves is rising. In a few days the coyotes will strip it down to hide and bones, and in a few months the grass will grow through the gaps in its rib cage. What's worse is when a cow refuses to leave her dead calf. Some of them stay for two or three days, wild-eyed and ready to defend, driven by a fearsome kind of love.

Half an hour of looking and we haven't found a thing. We walk the bush by the lake three times and the whole pasture once, which isn't easy because most of it is hillside, marked by stones and gullies. I find a sun-warmed rock and sit for a minute, thinking about how we might have missed the calf.

Jarvis (who doesn't care about damp ground) stretches out on the grass beside me. It's warm enough to be without a coat, without a sweatshirt even, the sun warm on our backs through our t-shirts.

"It's got to be somewhere in the bush," I say. "Are you sure you checked right down to the water?"

No answer.

I look at him, lying there with his arm raised up to block the sun, his eyes closed. I reach out to poke him in the ribs or push against his bent knee, to make the kind of contact we've made for years, but something happens. The clear, warm light strikes the metal of his belt buckle. My hand hesitates, mid-air, then my fingers relax, drift down and lie gentle on the buckle. His body shifts slightly, and I can feel the tightening of his muscles. He stares at me, a band of shadow across his eyes like a mask. I look at where his blue shirt covers his flat stomach, look lower, then up again at the hand resting between the two places, the hand that seems part of someone else, not mine at all. He moves his arm and curves his fingers around my wrist without pressure, not guiding my hand further, not pushing it away. A smell of sweet poplar buds blows up from the bush by the lake. I feel the rise and fall of his breathing, once, twice, before I lift my hand and Jarvis lets me go.

"Did you check right down to the water?" I ask again, rough-voiced, as if there had been no touching.

On our last trip across the hill, Jarvis spots the calf. All that can be seen are the tips of its ears. The cow had given birth at the edge of a deep, narrow gully full of melt water and rotten snow. The calf had slipped down into it and is buried up to the neck. We pull it out. Still breathing. Jarvis carries it home on his shoulders, not talking, quiet for once beneath the weight of something saved.

———

There are times, just as I wake from sleep or when I'm in the shower, eyes closed against the drum of water, times fewer with each passing year, when I wonder, What does Jarvis think about now? I'd like to get him alone on a school bus again. I'd beckon him close and whisper, The story goes like this. Would he listen? Would he recognize the words?

Forest and rock, forest and rock all around. The neon sign in front of the bar has been turned off for over an hour, but a few people linger long past closing. The talk, low and disjointed, is of journeys made or yet to be made to places beyond the narrow streets and miles of trees. There is talk of dreams. The room is dim, made even dimmer by a haze of sweet-smelling smoke. A young man cups a harmonica to his mouth and plays an awkward tune of his own devising. He is thin and stringy, the muscles in his arms visible as they move against the bones beneath them. The woman wears a shirt that is loose and gauzy, no bra, some beads. In the back pocket of her jeans she carries a small notepad to jot down the words she wants to keep. She is fascinated by the way he tongues the instrument, flutters his hand over it like a single-winged bird. Each note travels her body's surface before settling low in her belly. The weight of the music makes her move slowly as she gets up, goes to sit cross-legged next to him. She reaches out, lays a hand on him. The touch is like electricity. A jolt. Transformer man, she whispers, and he does not forget that phrase.

I want to hear Jarvis say, Yes, yes, that's how I remember it too.

The Weaning Season

Roy Lafonde has a reputation for being a somewhat unlucky man. Trees fall more often on his fences, summer showers bypass his fields, and his cows give birth to calves that refuse to suck. Back in '97, the same year the Eyehill school closed and Myra lost her job, a flurry of oil-related activity led to seismic testing on Roy's north quarter. The company drilled just one well, and it was sour. The yearly surface rights cheque seems especially small when the hydrogen sulfide emissions sink into the shallow valley where he built his house, and the smell of rotten eggs permeates the air of Myra's kitchen.

She looks out the window of that kitchen and watches Roy, Joseph and Roland sort cattle in the corral. The heads and shoulders of the brothers, the backs of the cows and the tops of the fence rails are dusted with snow, a few flakes still falling, even as the sun breaks through the clouds and slants over the farmyard from the west, lighting up the walls of the outbuildings with false warmth. Over two hundred cows bawling, over two hundred calves answering, bleats and bellows and occasionally something helpless and deep and enraged, a roar. The noise, like the sour gas, seems to penetrate the walls and windows of the house. Her head aches, just a little, where her skull meets her neck.

The job of separating the cows from their calves has used up most of the day. Myra has, as always, done her part. She cooks for the men — a pot of stew, pans of buns, racks of cookies —

turning the radio in the kitchen louder and louder as more cows are driven into one pen while their calves stay in the other. She should be happy, the sale of the calves is money after all, the culmination of a year's work. And once the weaning is done, Roy can service the tractor and the snow plow he uses for his winter job. He works for the same oil company that drilled the sour well, clearing snow drifts so tanker trucks can use the company roads to the leases carved out of his neighbours' fields. He'll be paid in the spring, another cheque signed by someone who sits at a desk in Calgary.

The door opens and Roy calls to her loudly, competing with the singer on the radio. She goes to the porch and sees him in the doorway, a tall man whose head almost touches the frame. Some grey shows in the dark hair that curls from under his cap. He is smiling, full of well-being on this day in November. Once the job is done, he and his brothers will drive to the beer parlour in town. Roy will buy the drinks. They will stay until it closes and eat potato chips and pickled eggs for supper. He asks Myra, as he does every year, if she would like to come to town with them. He expects her to say no and she always does, but every year he asks her anyway, out of consideration. His manners are better than those of the rest of the Lafondes. He keeps his elbows off the table. Because he married a school teacher, they all say, he eats like an educated man. It's one of the family's many jokes.

The advertisement had read: *Teacher wanted for small rural school to teach all subjects, grades one through three. Applicant must be willing to participate in extracurricular activities organized by the community. Experience not required.* The interview was held at the division office in Airedale. Myra did not even see Eyehill until after she was hired, the point of taking the job being not to go to Eyehill but to leave Saskatoon. She made the two-and-a-half-hour drive from the city in her father's car, the road dwindling from four lanes to two lanes to an ever-narrowing ribbon of gravel that wound its way alternately through unfarmable hills riven with gullies and pockets of ripening crop.

She met Roy when he came, with some of the fathers, to repair the backstop of the school's ball field, and she'd been impressed that a single man would want to spend his time that way. A few weeks later, when Joseph Lafonde caught them kissing in shadows of the back door of the Community Hall, he'd raised an eyebrow and said, Extracurricular activities? Another of the family's jokes. The night that Roy first kissed her, she'd been two days away from her twenty-third birthday. He was two years younger. Two years seemed like nothing then. She can't help but wonder, does Roy count them now?

The Lafondes are a big family, eight siblings, and all of them but Roy have produced at least one child. Some of these children are now giving birth to children of their own. Papa Émile used to say, laughing with his wife, We're good Catholics, eh, Mother? Some aunts and uncles still care enough about religion to say that for Roy there are no children because he married outside the faith. As the months and years pass, Roy looks at Myra sorry-eyed, and, if she asked, he would say he does not blame her. But he does. An only child, she lacks the evidence of brothers and sisters and fifty-three first cousins.

She leaves the kitchen, goes into the living room and watches through the picture window as the truck pulls out of the yard, glad to see the three men go. The cab is barely able to contain the bodies jammed inside, bodies that will touch all the way into town, a fifteen-minute drive, thighs rubbing side to side, arms flung around shoulders to make space. Myra has never seen any of them embrace, even when their mother, Eva, died painfully of gangrene. Émile and his sons simply faced each other, stiff-necked in dark blue ties, their bodies rigid with pain.

Myra has her own ritual for this day. She begins by putting the kettle on to boil. Outside, the sun sets, touches the faded planks of the corral with pink light. Just visible in the pen behind the barn is a restless, shifting mass of cattle. Tomorrow morning, a stock trailer will come to pick up the calves. The cows will not stop bawling all night, will keep it up through the next day and even the night after that. Myra knows this because one year there was a heavy rain, and the truck hired to pick up the calves could not make the trip over the slippery hills. The cows had not quieted through the long day of waiting for the truck. When it finally arrived the next morning, some cows still bawled hoarsely, stronger-voiced than the others, unable to forget.

She puts on a winter coat, takes an old sheep's wool comforter outside and sits on the veranda. Wrapped in the heavy wool, she will be able to sit for hours without feeling much cold. The noise does not pause, rises and falls depending on the number of cows calling for their calves at any given moment. Twelve years, she's bundled herself up and listened. The view changes: one of three old granaries collapsed last winter beneath heavy snow; the year before that, the mountain ash tree was toppled in an electrical storm by the same fierce wind that tore the cupola off the barn roof. Further in the distance, the flare that burns off the sour gas flickers in the sky. But the noise from the corrals never varies. Myra cannot find order in it, has never been able to, in all her years of listening.

When she married Roy, she had not expected this. She did not grow up on a farm, and for her the meat on her table was no different from other foods, something she paid for with money. Roy will survey a hot meal spread before him and say, Ah, Myra, vegetables from our own garden, beef from our own grass, and who knows? Some of the wheat in that bread could be from the field just up the road. He enjoys it all the more, knowing their sweat and worry helped to produce it. Myra, on the other hand, has grown thinner on the farm. The first November of her marriage, this weaning time took her by surprise. She dropped a plate and cut herself on the sharp pieces. Roy had come in to see if dinner was ready and found her on the floor in tears, blood dripping, a dishtowel held tightly against her mouth.

She knows she is not to blame because there are no children, could give reasons, but she says nothing, even though the silence grows harder to keep each year, especially since Bernice Lisgaard down the road told her about how their daughter, the one she and her husband Carl adopted nineteen years ago, wants to search for her mother. Birth mother is what they call it, Bernice said, they let kids like my Sara look for their birth mothers when they're old enough. Give them the papers and everything. Myra had nearly dropped the full cup of coffee she was passing to Bernice. That's how nerves affect her; they show in her hands, not her face. And the Saretsky girl, Suzy, who lives just down the road. Unmarried, two children, pregnant with a third, all with different fathers. Myra wonders if her hands tremble and drop crockery.

Myra sips her tea as the day grows rapidly darker. Old Émile can light a candle for his lost wife. There is a grave to visit. Myra does not have these things, but she has this noise-filled night when she can allow herself to remember the small portion she has left. The sickness that did not go away after three months like they said it would. The heaviness, the flattened feeling in the bottoms of her feet. The restless movements within her as the baby turned. At family gatherings, she listens to the La-fonde women talk of childbirth, of the pain that is forgotten the moment a newborn takes the breast. They talk freely until one of them remembers Myra is there. Then they change the subject, as if she were a child who had been carelessly let in on something beyond her understanding.

But Myra knows about the pain. She would like to say to these women, I have not forgotten what it was like when my body was a fist clenched, the feeling when at last the fist opened. I don't even know if the baby was a boy or girl, she could say. She used to walk about the classroom, teaching the youngest children how to sound out words, moving on, as they got older, to the shaping of letters, the multiplication tables, long division, the names of the Great Lakes, thinking, until her own lost child's age overtook that of the children bent over their desks: that one could be mine. At the last gathering of Lafondes, when she marvelled, as she was expected to, at the intelligence of this niece or that nephew, at how fast they were growing, at their athletic prowess, what she wanted to say was, My child will be fifteen years old in December. What she really wants to say is *my child*.

The sun disappeared completely some time ago, and it should be very dark, but the sky is clear, and the light of a half-moon is reflected and intensified by the snow. She can make out the shapes of animals in the corral. Words threaten to spill out; she is a container too small to hold the phrases. More in sorrow than in anger. Who said that? The words sound of judgment, of something a parent or a preacher might have said. Wrong. She feels the opposite, more anger, Myra is angrier now than she was then. What had they told her? There will be other children, later on, when you can give them the family they deserve. Lots of time. She had let them make the arrangements, and (there must be honesty, tonight of all nights) she had felt, among all the other things, relief.

Good thing the teacup is almost empty, because her hands have started to shake. It is late, Roy will soon be home, and she should go to bed, be asleep or at least pretending when he gets back. Otherwise she might tell him everything, and what good would that do? He would be hurt, maybe not believe her when she tells him she doesn't regret the father, just the child. The father is a dim memory of fumbling and giving in and a quick-ly, crookedly buttoned blouse. Knowing about that long-ago child might make Roy start to blame himself for the fact that there are no children now, and really, she tells herself, no one is to blame.

It seems hardly possible, but the noise is louder than before. Myra wants to throw back her head and mingle her own long cries with those of the cattle. But she can't give in. She's learned that much, at least. Giving in isn't just for an hour or a day. Jaws clamped together, lips pressed tight, she slips out of the warm space beneath the comforter. She walks around the piece of grass between the house and barn, picking up a rake and propping it against the trunk of a tree, collecting the sticks the dog drags up to the house, tidying, moving without thinking, getting closer and closer to the dark shapes in the corral.

Most days, she is afraid of the animals, of their size and un-expected passion. She has watched Roy try to take a newborn calf from its mother and move it to the warmth of the barn. The cow put down its head and bellowed, ran Roy right over the fence, had him scrambling to reach the other side. Roy wasn't hurt, wasn't angry even. When he'd seen Myra's white face, he'd tried to comfort her. That's nature, he said. Natural behaviour. And Myra was ashamed.

She is just a few feet away from the corral. The cows and calves are penned side by side, a sturdy fence of old railway ties and two-by-eights between them, the gate closed tight with a loop of chain. Some of the cows closest to the fence cease their bawling and look at her. She takes a few steps closer, thinking she might touch one of the animals through the spaces between the boards and comfort it. Her fingers, reaching out, stroke the coarse hair. My baby, she whispers, then louder, my child. The cow takes up the chant for her, bellows her want in a voice that carries a quarter mile.

Myra's husband has had too much to drink, but even so he knows as soon as he pulls into the yard, before he even gets out of the truck, that something has changed. There is too much noise. Not the sound of bawling, which is what he expects to hear, but the deep pounding sound of cattle on the move. He puts his foot down hard on the gas pedal, spraying gravel from the back wheels as he drives the short distance down to the corral. Roy Lafonde catches his wife in the headlights' glare, her hand steady on the open gate, the cattle streaming past her, cows and calves reunited. Her lips are moving. She can't hear her, but she's speaking. Shouting her answer to the question no one has ever thought to ask.

Updraft

Queer, even for a McEnry. That's what they said in the town where he grew up. His habit as a child was to stand with his arms stretched straight out from his shoulders, chin lifted to the sky, circling and circling slowly, until he fell to the ground. He did this in the middle of Main Street once and was almost hit by a truck. He was also known as the first of the McEnrys whose schooling went beyond the sixth grade. This did not please his father, who was convinced Bill clung to school as a way to avoid real work, but, as the old man was fond of saying, all good things must come to an end, and school in that town ran out at grade eight. So Bill went to work at the mill, and not much was said about him for several years. Then, when he was a young man less than two years married, he disappeared, leaving behind a wife and baby daughter. People said he was dead, his body scavenged by wild animals; the coyotes were particularly hungry that year. They said he'd run off with another woman, despite the fact that old Mrs. Cuthbert took particular care to inventory all the women in the town and surrounding area the next day, and all were accounted for. The station master said he'd seen him by the train tracks waiting for the chance to hop a freight, but the station master was a drunk, well known for seeing things, so he was ignored. Some said, he'll find out the hard way, he'll be back. But he didn't come back. The people who had watched him when he was a boy, spinning slowly round and round, never heard from him again.

Rudy finally hits a green light at the last intersection, and he guns the motor of his less than new Accord, guns it just a little, because he is a vice principal, and sure as hell if he is stopped by the police, the cop will turn out to be the father of one of his students. The budget meeting went two hours over schedule. He's late for supper, hungry, tired and still not sure what he wants to say about the condom. His heart is fluttering queerly in his chest.

Last night when he got home from work, his wife, looking wide-eyed and bothered, met him at the door, motioning for him to follow her to the bedroom. She closed the door, turned the lock and offered him the small foil package she found in their oldest daughter's jacket pocket.

"What should we do?" she asked. "Should we be glad she's thinking of protection?"

Rudy looked at it. "Do you want to talk to her?"

"I'll cry. You know what I'm like."

Rudy pulls up to his stuccoed bungalow, noticing that the dandelions have renewed their invasion of the small cracks in the asphalt of the driveway. Twice, so far, he thought he'd rooted them out. He parks in the garage, enters the porch through the connecting door, and sees his wife bent over the kitchen counter, rolling pastry. She turns and jerks her chin toward the living room. The girls are in there, watching TV.

In the bedroom, he changes into a pair of jeans tagged Relaxed Fit, puts the condom into his pocket, and heads outside, nodding again in response to his wife's raised eyebrows as he passes. He sits on the ground, on the side of the garage hidden from view of the house, leaning back against the clapboard ridges. The sky above the rowanberry is grey with clouds left over from the morning's rain, and for some reason, perhaps

because of the earlier palpitations in his chest, he thinks of
Uncle Bill, who died of a heart attack when Rudy was fifteen.

He was related to Rudy, not by blood, but by marriage to
Aunt Lou, who was past forty at the time, the sister who'd
stayed home to look after her parents. When they died, Lou
carried on with the farming, and one day, a salesman stopped
at her farm to try to sell her a set of encyclopedias. Did you
know the human body is more than eighty-five percent water?
he'd asked. Come in, she said, you're letting in the cold. That's
how Aunt Lou met William McEnry. They lived together for
years on a farm a few miles north of Eyehill, and it became
legend in the district how Aunt Lou farmed the land, sat out
in the heat and wind on a cabless tractor, while her husband
stayed in the house, watching *The Edge of Night*. When the soap
opera was over, Uncle Bill boiled the kettle or cracked ice cubes
out of a tray, depending on the weather, and took Lou a drink.
She'd stop the tractor for a while and he'd tell her about the
characters on TV, about who was in love with whom and who
left whom and who put a poisonous spider in a rival's bed.
Rudy remembers seeing them together that way through the
school bus window, Bill leaning against a wheel, Lou sitting
in the tractor seat, both of them smiling.

Moisture from the damp lawn seeps into the ass of Rudy's
pants. He looks down, shifts, pulls the condom out of his pocket, and examines the way it takes up space in the palm of his
hand, trying to think of good reasons. Why he should not talk
to his daughter. Why he should pretend to his wife that he has.

To Ellie, Eyehill is just a name on the black schedule board at
the bus depot — Saskatoon, Airedale, Eyehill — the last stop on
the run. But she is going there, by God, and there is no one
going to stop her. Ellie hasn't left the city in years, doesn't even
like leaving the hotel where she lives and pays for her room by
the month. She's had three or four drinks already, and there's a

bottle in her purse just in case she loses her nerve. A young girl, maybe nineteen or twenty, sits across from her on one of the benches, waiting, like Ellie, for the bus. The girl has a small suitcase and another bag filled with books. She is reading one of them and making notes. I could have been like her, Ellie thinks, if things had been different. I could have been a veterinary assistant. She has always been fond of animals, putting out dishes of milk for the stray cats that wander through the alley behind the hotel.

The last twenty years of her life have been spent in the Imperial Hotel, under various circumstances. When she was a young girl, a newcomer to the city, she got a job cleaning rooms there. It was not a fancy place, even then, but it was decent. You could get a meal and a firm mattress. During the week, the rooms were rented by businessmen, salesmen mostly, who were slightly below average in their success. She and another chambermaid named Beryl supplemented their wages by providing the men with extras, starting with a back scrub for a dollar and going up from there. Nothing wrong with it. Just a service, like making a bed or hanging clean towels. She and Beryl took turns, dividing business equally. One night a fellow who'd been at the hotel a few times before but never asked for extras called the switchboard for a chambermaid. He was young and polite, with chances for success still ahead of him. It was Beryl's turn. Three weeks later, the young man and Beryl were married by a JP, and Beryl left the Imperial forever. If it'd been my turn, Ellie thinks, who knows what roads I might have travelled? After Beryl's marriage, Ellie seemed to spend most of her time in the rooms of men who had bottles. Men poured her drinks and she drank with gratitude. The dark liquid in the cheap hotel glass was a gift, something separate from the money they left under the pillow for her to pocket when she cleaned the room the next morning.

The departure of the bus to Airedale and Eyehill is announced. She watches the young girl close her book and stand up. Ellie straightens, imitating the girl's good posture. She checks her pockets nervously, feels the bus ticket, then the thin sheet of newsprint. Her father's obituary. If he hadn't taken off, she thinks, I might have had a different life.

Rudy found the hawk chick in the middle of a field. Right in the middle of a field just plowed for planting, not a tree for a quarter mile. It didn't have any feathers, just soft white patches of down, and it looked dead, eyes closed, tongue sticking out swollen and black. He poked the bird gently with a stick. It jerked a leg. He threw his jacket over it and scooped it up to take home.

His mother said it wouldn't live, her bleak prediction perhaps brought on by his father's death just that winter past. He'd died of pneumonia at a time when it seemed nobody died of that anymore, so Rudy's mother was pessimistic. What does it need, he asked, who knows what a hawk chick eats?

If it had been a sick calf or a lame horse, she would have told him to talk to Wally Bodnar, a farmer up the road. But this was a hawk.

She said, finally, Ask Uncle Bill.

People called him Britannica Bill: he'd sold encyclopedias before he married Lou, and he knew so much about things that others never thought of. School children called him regularly for help with their reports. What's the winter home of butterflies? they'd ask.

An eyedropper for water, he said, and meat for later, if the chick survives the night. He came over and looked into the straw-lined box, saw the chick tipped over on its back, too weak to stand. They dripped water onto the black tongue. In the morning, the bird was still alive. It opened its eyes and looked around. Uncle Bill dropped by again that night, and they fed the chick ground beef. He brought a pair of long tweezers and showed Rudy how to use them to feed the bird without getting pecked. Uncle Bill said, By the time this is over, you will know things that others don't. Not many people, boys or men, have watched a hawk grow wings.

Ellie watches the young girl with the books get off the bus at Airedale. Her parents are there to pick her up. Her father carries her suitcase to the car. Ellie feels it rise up, the bitterness that is as much a part of her as her own two arms and legs. She has not had advantages. Her mother often used that phrase when Ellie spoke of new skates, or money being collected at school for a teacher's year-end gift, or piano lessons. Now Ellie, she'd say, with your father gone we don't have those advantages. You have to do your part, her mother said.

The bus manoeuvres through the narrow space between gas pumps and parked cars, turns left onto the street leading to the highway and Eyehill. The times when she is hungry are the times she is most likely to think of her father. She gets out of her seat, heads for the bathroom at the back of the bus, feeling the weight of the rum bottle in her purse. She has less appetite after a few drinks. She has used this method for years and recommends it to friends who want to keep their figures.

Rudy and his mother were at Aunt Lou's house the day Bill's daughter came to the door. He felt too old to leave the women to their coffee and go down to the lake to skip stones, and too young to be their equal in conversation. And too awkward. The talk was of Uncle Bill, dead just a few months, and there were no easy words for the memory of him.

The woman who knocked on the door was neither young nor old. She might have been Rudy's mother's age, but she wore her hair long, and his mother and his friends' mothers did not. He was, by then, old enough to notice the habits of women, and he saw that her makeup, too, was different. Women of his mother's age wore lipstick when they went out, nothing else. This woman's lips were pale, her eyes painted with thick black lines, like the girls at school who traced their eyelids with dark pencil. Rudy stood up that day and offered Bill McEnry's daughter his chair at the table. It wasn't just good manners. Something in him hoped for the chance to get away, but the woman did not want to sit, so he remembers standing with her while she talked. Her name was Eleanor. Eleanor McEnry.

He left us, she said, and me just a tiny baby, only three months old. Mother said she woke up in the morning and I was quiet in my crib and he was gone. A good-for-nothing, like she'd been warned about. She got a job cooking and keeping house for a neighbour man. We lived with him for a while, then one morning she threw a dishtowel in his face and we left that afternoon. There were other men she cooked for after that. All to give me a home.

That summer was the first time Rudy ever tasted rum. One of the guys had found his father's bottle hidden in the machine shed, about half full. As Eleanor McEnry spoke, the room filled with the sweet smell of Captain Morgan's Dark.

You'll never believe how I found him, she said. At the hairdresser's. Turns out the woman who cuts my hair grew up here. Her mother gives her a subscription to the paper every year for Christmas. While I was waiting under the dryer, I look at this paper and I see the name, right there at the top of the obituaries, William McEnry, mourned by his wife. No kids. Never had another kid but me. So I think you owe me something, you people. I think I'm entitled.

Aunt Lou gave the woman twenty thousand dollars. Just like that. Wrote her a cheque and offered her a cup of coffee. On the short drive home, Rudy remembers his mother struggling to make sense of it.

"What if that woman is a liar, a fake? What if she is no relation at all?"

"She looked a bit like him. Her face, from the eyes down."

"Suppose she is his daughter. What kind of man leaves his family, just like that?"

When Rudy's oldest daughter, the sixteen-year-old, the one with the condom in her jacket pocket, was three weeks old, she began to cry and continued to cry for hours at a time for no apparent reason. They lived in a cheap apartment close to the railway tracks, and one night, when there was no sound from her crib for an hour and a half, when even a passing train did not wake her, he and his exhausted wife let themselves drift into sleep.

He was awakened, soon after, not by the baby, but by his wife. She lifted her hands in two clasped fists and brought them down on him, drove them high into his belly below the sternum, knocking the breath out of him.

"Baby's crying," she hissed.

He'd stumbled out of the bed to obey, stupid and amazed by the violent awakening. The baby was certainly crying, and she didn't stop when he entered the room, not even when he picked her up and sat to rock her, holding her close to the tender, hollow place where his wife's fists had landed. Her eyes were closed, her mouth open. He rocked, she cried, steadily, out of rhythm with the rocker and his heartbeat. He felt the panic rising. He thought of being a junior high science teacher for the rest of his life, the students less and less interested as the years wore on, the principal saying, I'd like you to sit on this committee and this one and this one. He thought of his wife, her eyes dull with lack of sleep and laughter, her voice sharpening into a whine. His daughter cried on, a screaming weight in his lap, and suddenly, fiercely, he wanted to pick her up and swing her in two swift circles and let go, let her go sailing out the third-storey window, let the frozen ground break her crying. He started to rise, stopped. Breathe deep, Rudy, breathe deep.

He said it out loud. The baby sucked in her breath, held it. The tail end of a train whistle sounded in the brief silence.

A wind has come up, and though the garage wall shelters him a little, the leftover eddies and gusts of air make the place where Rudy sits drafty and cold. Above him, the clouds are moving, shifting layers of grey, some light, some dark. The summer he and Uncle Bill saved the hawk chick started him sky watching. Three times a day, they scanned the horizon, trying to judge wind and clouds, trying to know what a hawk would know about when the time was right for flying.

The back door opens, releasing the smell of cinnamon and cherry pie. His wife cooks when she's feeling nervous or grateful, and tonight the thought of him taking care of the condom likely gives rise to both emotions. She is looking for him, but he's hidden from view by the cedar tree.

"Rudy?" she whispers.

He stays quiet, sits still, and after a moment, the door closes.

Uncle Bill's was a sudden death that led to more talk than usual in Eyehill because of the irony. In those days, it was generally believed that heart attacks were caused by hard work or worry or excess weight. Uncle Bill was thin and easy-going. Never did a full day's work in his life, the neighbours used to say. Even so, he was a burly man, his arms thick and strong at the shoulder. Rudy was small enough that even though the older man knelt, one knee on the ground, his head rested against Bill's chest and his eyes ran level with the arm that dwindled to a single raised finger, a finger that pointed to a hawk being chased by a flock of smaller birds.

"Look, Rudy, see how they catch up to him, even though his wings are so much bigger? That's because a hawk depends on wind. His wings are made for gliding."

The hawk flapped, tried to glide, flapped again, the pointed beaks pursuing him. Suddenly, he shot upward, just like magic, far away from the flock and getting farther, until he was just a speck in the sky.

"Caught the updraft," Uncle Bill said. "A lucky wind."

Rudy gets up, his legs a little stiff from the damp ground. No use putting it off any longer.

Across the alley, above his neighbours' houses, the clouds are separating and the sun shines through them, like it does sometimes, showing itself as visible columns of light. He cracks the door open an inch or two, and the music from his daughters' favourite game show drifts into the back yard.

It is nearly dark by the time Ellie leaves the bus depot to go to her room at the hotel. Walking down the city street beside the cars, their lights sharp in her eyes, she recalls the afternoon, the awkward kindness of Lou, the way the boy offered her a chair, the flash of red bird wing less real than the blink of tail lights in front of her. But the cheque is real, doubled over in her pocket.

The possibilities of twenty thousand dollars. She could afford an apartment, take a course, find a job. She walks faster, her feet trying to keep pace with the choices offered by her new life. Already she can see the bright sign over the hotel where she has a room on the third floor. She feels a strange, spreading weightlessness, a lifting that threatens to float her, spin her in slow circles above the city. Frightened, she stops by the bar that occupies the first floor of the hotel. Just one drink. That's all she needs to combat this frightening buoyancy beneath her arms.

She still can't believe it, can't believe that woman, Lou. Sitting there at the kitchen table in a man's jack shirt and green work pants, writing a cheque for twenty thousand. When it was time for Ellie to go, Lou said she would drive her into town. She did not offer stories about Bill McEnry, except to say, when the car passed a slough and a flock of red-winged blackbirds rose up out of the cattails, Your father imitated bird calls. He could whistle an oriole right up to the house. You couldn't tell him from the real thing.

Social Graces

The four of us are sitting around the kitchen table looking down at bowls of a horrible thing called bread pudding. Bread is for grilled cheese sandwiches and toast and soaking up gravy. It is not a dessert. Aunt Charlotte is responsible for it, as she is for the orange pill that waits on my plate every night at supper.

"Every year," she says, "I write to your father asking him to send you to stay with us in Winnipeg for the Christmas holidays, and every year, I am told that you are sick with the flu and unable to travel. A normal, healthy girl does not suffer from influenza on a regular basis."

She passes more bread pudding to my father.

"Louise takes her vitamin every day. I see to it."

Plump Louise eats her pudding. She has dark brown hair, the same colour as mine, but much longer. Her mother puts it up in curlers on Saturday nights so it will fall in ringlets for church on Sunday. The curlers are made of wire and stiff bristles and must hurt, but Louise, perhaps tougher than she looks, never complains.

"Rhea has a bad chest," my father says. This is a lie. I almost never get sick, except for the time I got chicken pox in grade three, and that shouldn't count against me. Every kid in Eyehill had them.

"Perhaps that's why she's so thin." Aunt Charlotte finishes her bread pudding and dabs her lips with one of the cloth napkins she brought with her in her suitcase. Louise is just a year older than I am, but she already wears a brassiere. When she takes it off at night, there is a red line across her back where the elastic irritates the skin.

The house has been full of noise since their arrival. Aunt Charlotte wears hard-soled shoes, and her footsteps clack on the linoleum. The electric hand mixer whines, pots clang, and at least once a day she says, Sing for us, Louise, and then the girl starts in, her voice pitched high above the scrape of her mother's spoon against the mixing bowl.

> *My bonnie lies over the ocean,*
> *My bonnie lies over the sea . . .*

I never see my father during the day. Early in the morning, he packs sandwiches and a thermos of coffee, and he doesn't come back to the house until nearly suppertime, when it's starting to get dark. Roxanna and I can't cut snowflake stencils for the windows and spray them with the sticky snow that comes in a can because Aunt Charlotte is here. Aunt Charlotte, who tells me to chew with my mouth closed, to take the stairs one at a time, to cross my ankles when seated. There never was a Mc-Curdy without the social graces, she says, and as long as I draw breath, there will never be one.

After supper, we watch television, a Jacques Cousteau deep-sea adventure. I like how the divers return to the surface in slow motion, their bodies an undulating chain of S-curves as they ascend. The announcer explains that a man who rises too quickly will suffer painful bends. Sharks drift past but they are friendly, as long as there is no blood in the water.

"I'm bored," Louise whispers to her mother.

Aunt Charlotte gives her a look, then pretends she hasn't heard. Whispering is bad manners. That's what I was told earlier in the week. My father reaches into the magazine rack beside his chair and passes Louise a book, *Riders of the Purple Sage*. He read it to me last winter. I could read it for myself, but

I like the way he does it, the drawl he gives the characters, the high voice he puts on when the heroine speaks.

Her mother frowns at the cover, then looks at my father.

"Alphonse?"

"Charlotte?"

"Is there much shooting in that book? Much bloodshed?"

He shakes his head. Another lie. The rustler, Oldring, is shot straight through the heart by Venters.

Aunt Charlotte nods her permission for Louise to open it, then continues to darn her way through a pile of socks. She slips an empty water glass into the foot of one of them, positioning the hole in the sock's heel over the mouth of the glass and weaving the worn edges together. The wool makes very little sound as it slips through the sock. Her clacking feet rest silently on a stool.

I tiptoe out of the room, wearing the same clothes as yesterday, so as not to wake Louise by opening the squeaky dresser drawers. My father is sitting at the kitchen table, eating cold bread and jam, unwilling to risk the loud pop of the toaster. He butters two more slices for me, puts the sticky sides together, and motions for us to go outside.

The slough where the horses drink is covered with a thick layer of ice. Every morning, my father chops a hole so they can get at the water. He lifts a special tool, a heavy metal bar with an axe head welded to the end of it, and braces himself, feet apart, over the place where, every day, the hole grows a new skin of ice. He positions the long metal bar in front of him, axe head pointing downward. His hands stop just above his head in their lifting, and then he lets the axe fall. Ice chips fly and skitter away over the frozen surface, tinkling a little, like the wind chimes that hang above the post office door.

The horses come, pausing for a minute at the crest of the small hill that slopes down to the slough. They descend slowly, picking their way through the thin layer of snow. The roan mare limps behind the others.

"You finish," he says, handing me the axe. "You've watched me enough times to know how."

He walks toward the lame mare.

I lift the heavy axe head and let it drop. A few ice chips break away from the ragged edges of the hole. Lift, drop, lift again, a rhythm more clumsy than my father's but a rhythm nonetheless. After a while, the fragments of ice that fly from the hole carry some water with them, a sign that the best part will happen soon. One, two, three, four more blows of the axe, and the water gushes up to meet the blade, gurgling a little. I sweep the axe head in a sideways motion, clearing the water of bits of ice left over from the chopping, sloshing it over my boots. This winter water is very green, not blue like it is in summer. The black gelding, Lefty, walks carefully over the few feet of ice and puts his nose to the hole.

When we get home, Aunt Charlotte calls me into the bedroom, where Louise is sitting on the edge of the bed.

"Please, Rhea, sit down."

Both of them have funny looks on their faces. Louise looks a little sick but triumphant, like a person who just won first place in a hot-dog eating contest. Aunt Louise is solemn, the look on her face like that of Mrs. Bostwick, the postmistress, when she hands out prizes at the Eyehill School Oratory Contest.

"Louise is having quite a day," Aunt Charlotte says.

How? She's still in her pyjamas.

"This morning, Louise began her menses."

Oh god. Another type of song?

"Do you know what that means, Rhea?"

I shake my head.

"She has changed from girl to woman. Rather sooner than I expected. It will happen to you, perhaps before too long,

which is why Louise and I are sharing this with you. There may
not be a another woman around when your turn comes."

"Roxanna is usually here."

"Roxanna. Yes. Well, in any case . . ."

Aunt Charlotte sits on the cot, facing me. She takes Louise's
hand in one of hers and mine in the other.

"There is blood, but it's perfectly natural, and there's less
than a cupful, I'm told, if you were to actually measure it.
Carry on with life as usual or everyone will know, and your
menses are strictly private. Men should be kept out of it
altogether."

She releases her hold on our hands, and the next ten minutes are spent in a demonstration of the equipment necessary
to keep the secret. Louise does not look perfectly natural. Once
her mother leaves the room, she looks ready to throw up, and
I feel a little sorry for the times I whispered *Lou-sneeze, Lou-
pees*, behind her back.

That afternoon, Aunt Charlotte washes Louise's hair and wraps
her head in a towel. Tomorrow is the Sunday before Christmas.
She gets the bag of rollers, and Louise holds them in her lap,
passing them to her mother one at a time. A section of hair is
combed out straight and smooth, then rolled up tightly and
secured with a straight, sharp pin made of white plastic. When
she is finished, Aunt Charlotte washes her hands and takes
a fresh pan of bread pudding out of the oven. If prayers are
answered, it will be the last. On Monday, she and Louise are
going back to Winnipeg, where Louise's father is one of the men
who make the Eaton's catalogue. They will be home in time for
Christmas Eve.

My father and I watch the hockey game, which is a more
complicated activity than usual because Boston is playing Toronto. Bobby Orr is the problem. I cheer for the Canadian

teams out of a sense of loyalty to my own kind, but Bobby Orr, everyone knows, is a hero whose grace and courage should rightly earn a win. So I cheer for Toronto out loud and for Bobby in my head.

Louise sits in the big chair, her face hidden behind the dull green cover of *Riders of the Purple Sage*. I wonder if she has reached the part where Lassiter shoots the crooked Mormons who want to take Jane's land.

Louise and I are sent to bed once the hockey game is over. The sound of Tommy Hunter's guitar comes through the long curtain that divides the bedroom from the living room. I always go right to sleep, but tonight two things keep me awake: Louise, turning restlessly from side to side, and the need to eavesdrop on the conversation Aunt Charlotte is having with my father.

"Come now, Alphonse. Surely you see she's at the age when a young girl needs a woman's guidance. She and Louise would be company for one another."

I strain to hear my father's reply, but his low voice is drowned out by the guitar and by the muffled sound of Louise crying into her pillow.

"Think about it," Aunt Charlotte says. "I won't ask again."

Louise is still crying. I slip over to the cot.

"I'm homesick," Louise says. "My stomach hurts."

"Sit up for a minute."

Louise does as she is told. I remove the rollers, unwinding them slowly because I'm unused to the procedure, and I can't see well in the dark. The strands of hair are still damp.

"Mom will have a fit."

"We'll put them back in the morning before she's awake. What you don't know can't hurt you, that's what Roxanna says."

Louise sits very still until the last roller is out. Then she asks, "If you were Jane, would you ride off with Lassiter?"

"Yes."

"But he's a killer. He kills a man."

"Some people need to be shot. That's the point."

"Would you want him to roll the stone that sealed the canyon, trapping the two of you there forever, not even married?"

"I'd rather be Lassiter," I say. "I'd like to roll the stone myself."

On Monday morning, we drive Aunt Charlotte and Louise to Airedale, where they will catch the eastbound train to Winnipeg. It is snowing a little, but the four of us stand outside, sheltered by the over-hanging roof. Aunt Charlotte says this is the last truly fresh air she and Louise will breathe for several hours. She looks for a long moment at me.

"Perhaps you'll come to Winnipeg someday," she says.

"Maybe. If my health improves."

The train will soon be leaving. A man in uniform comes for Aunt Charlotte and Louise's suitcases. My father takes a bag of mints out of his pocket and passes it to Louise.

"For the trip," he says.

"Thank you."

He shifts his position a step or two, until his body is positioned directly behind mine. He places his hands lightly on my shoulders, drawing me back to rest against his legs, looking over my head at Aunt Charlotte.

I don't want to be outdone, in manners or anything else, by Louise.

"Thank you for . . ." I hesitate, not sure how to finish. "Thank you for taking the trouble." That's what Mrs. Bostwick says when my father gives her a ride back to the post office from the store. When a neighbour drops in, my father always sees him to the door at the end of the visit, and the last thing he says is, Come again, anytime.

"Goodbye, Charlotte."

I wait for more, but that's all he says.

Every year in early December, a parcel arrives from Winnipeg. Inside is a diary with a locked metal clasp, a tiny key and a note exhorting me to keep a record of my days. It is the only contact I have, beyond that one never-to-be-repeated visit, with Charlotte Pearson, née McCurdy, my runaway mother's older and more settled sister.

Practical Women

The worst part of Noreen's job is that she has to wear panty-hose. The ones she pulled on this morning are too small; the crotch binds her legs together almost to the knee, and the nylon clings to every surface of skin. The feeling reminds her of a boy she used to date in high school, the type of boy who had to be peeled off. The doors of the Airedale Pioneer Seniors' Lodge are made of glass, and as she approaches, she sees, through her own white-uniformed reflection, the face of one of the residents watching her arrival. She can't say which, because she hasn't yet learned, as Beryl has, to differentiate among faces so alike in their wrinkles, so much the same in their sag.

"Just like your daddy," the old woman says, as Noreen passes by. The random comments of the elderly are something else she has to adjust to. She can't continue to be startled by words that come out of nowhere.

"Beautiful morning," Noreen says.

"The noise woke me."

"Oh. What noise?"

"Is today the fourteenth?"

"Yes."

"Of July?"

"Yes."

"Jeannie's coming tomorrow."

"That's nice."

"My son's daughter."

"Nice to have a visitor," Noreen says, and leaves the old woman standing by the door. On her way to the kitchen, she pauses by the menu board in front of the dining hall, admiring the curves of letters she printed yesterday. Breakfast: soft-boiled egg. Lunch: creamed peas on toast. Dinner: shepherd's pie, raspberry Jell-O. Noreen prints beautifully, everyone says so, and it is her job to write the daily menus on the clean, white board. Down in the corner, she drew a small sheep and a man with a shepherd's crook. No one has told her not to draw on the board, but she suspects that too much of it would be against the rules. She hurries toward the kitchen, where Beryl and the others are preparing breakfast.

The old woman stands in the largeness of the foyer. The view to the west is the green vinyl seats of visitors' chairs and the letters on the menu board. To the east, there is sunlight on the sparrows' wings as they pass by the glass door. *Morning, little ones, Momma's little ones, shh, shh, don't cry, sweet pea, give me a smile, there's a good baby. Are you going to grow up to be*

"Just like your daddy," the old woman says again.

Even though he has an assistant, hired to do the work of cleaning toilets and floors and windows, Dixon prefers to do the sweeping himself. He notices that Noreen, the new girl, wipes her feet on the mat when she comes in. The women who work at the lodge like Dixon because he fixes things for them, broken necklace clasps and toasters that always burn one side of the bread, things their husbands won't bother with. Noreen is walking towards him, her uniform clean and unwrinkled, on her way to the kitchen. She wears a hairnet, and the bundled hair inside is always centred on her neck, her face framed by equal halves of its brown shape. Dixon would like to touch the wonderful symmetry of this trapped hair. Unaware, she smiles and says, "Another nice day."

He nods, starting to sweat.

She disappears into the kitchen. He sweeps past the open door and hears her saying "Nice day" again, this time to a woman inside. A positive attitude, that's another thing he likes.

He makes his way to the foyer and sees Mrs. Powell looking out the glass doors. She pops up here and there at odd hours, more mobile, he suspects, than the nurses know.

"Are you married, Dixon?"

"Not that lucky, Mrs. Powell."

"Call me Vera. My granddaughter's coming tomorrow. She lives in Winnipeg."

"Didn't know you had a granddaughter."

"My son's girl. He died when she was a baby. Drowned. Late March, the ice is always rotten. You can't trust it."

"She been here before?"

"Not since she was a child."

"What brings her here?"

"She wants to know what killed her ancestors."

"Oh."

"It passes the time," Vera says, and moves aside so Dixon can keep sweeping. She watches his elbow bend and straighten as he pushes the broom.

The cream sauce for the peas is threatening to turn thick and gluey. Beryl glances into the pan on her way to the walk-in freezer.

"Needs more milk."

Noreen stirs, watching the older woman carry bags of frozen ground beef from the freezer to the stainless steel counter. Beryl is strong. She runs the kitchen, pointing orders with a thick finger. Her forearms bulge when she lifts the meat. She is in her sixties, thirty years older than Noreen, and has a daughter about Noreen's age who lives somewhere in Northern Ontario. The two don't get on, never have. The daughter left home at seventeen, ran off with a man Beryl didn't like.

"Were you upset?" Noreen had asked.

"Is a frog's ass watertight? Of course I was upset."

Noreen decides to change the subject.

"That's an interesting ring." The older woman wears an unusual wedding band, the gold carved with intricate patterns.

"My mother's. My father made it for her."

"It's beautiful."

"He was a goldsmith in the old country. Named all his girls after stones. I had a sister called Opal," Beryl points spoon toward the stove, indicating that Noreen should check the cream sauce. "They left Ireland in 1928, came out here just in time to starve during the Depression. When I was sixteen, I left the homestead and went to work at a hotel in Saskatoon."

When Noreen gets up, Beryl says, "Put the kettle on. We'll drink a cup of tea while we make the toast. Let the others set the tables." Four women work in the kitchen, but the other two are part-time, not good for much, Beryl says, but sorting cutlery and wiping tables.

Beryl polishes the ring with the corner of a dishtowel while they wait for the toast to pop. "My husband was a salesman, not a very good one, but I was young and thought that any man who owned two suits couldn't be too badly off. When we married, there was no money for a ring, so my mother gave me hers. Said she didn't need it anymore."

"Why?"

"My father was dead." Beryl takes a block of butter, slices it in half, puts each piece on a saucer.

"But didn't she —"

"Want to be buried with it? That's what I asked her." The toast pops, twelve slices at a time. Beryl butters each piece with a single pass of the knife, "Not too much butter, Noreen, it doesn't agree with them."

Noreen is still curious about the ring, but Beryl has moved on. "See much of Eddie these days?"

"He comes around."

"Is it serious?"

"He's still married."

Beryl refills the toaster. "Will there be a divorce?"

"He says so. Last week, he fixed her garage door, and this week he's rotating the tires on her van. The kids have got to be safe, he says."

Noreen gets up to give the cream sauce another stir. The hum of the toaster increases in volume. She knows Beryl has more to say. The sound of the toast popping acts like a signal.

"Maybe you should get rid of Eddie."

"Why?"

"What's in it for you? He ever look under the hood of your car?"

"No."

"You should think about the future. You want kids, don't you?"

"I don't know," Noreen says.

A janitor is cleaning the windows by the door when Jeannie arrives. The place seems decent enough. Jeannie's mother asked her to check on the care provided for her mother-in-law. Have a look at the food if you can, she said, and the sheets, see if they're clean. A desk near the front seems to be there for the purpose of providing information, but no one sits behind it. Several old people, most of them women, are gathered in an open area, a sort of lounge to the left of the foyer. Jeannie looks at them from the corner of her eye, wondering if her grandmother is among them. She wanders the foyer, unwilling and slightly afraid to go down the hallway looking in doors.

The clink of cutlery and glasses leads her to the dining room, where two women are clearing tables.

"I don't mind being on my own, if it doesn't work out with Eddie," one says to the other.

"Find a man who doesn't talk much, someone who's handy."

"Excuse me," Jeannie says, "I'm looking for a Mrs. Vera Powell."

The older woman, the one she interrupted, answers, "Take the first hallway on your left. Hers is the second room on the right." Jeannie starts in the direction indicated by the pointed finger, lengthening her steps a little in an attempt to avoid eavesdropping as the woman continues with her loud advice.

"Men who are all talk, I had one once and I wouldn't have another. Not if his pockets were lined with gold and his arse-hole studded with diamonds."

A young nurse's aide combs Vera's hair. The hairdresser who comes every Monday set it yesterday, and the curls are still there, flattened slightly on one side. *Comb dragged across scalp like cat's claws. Hair pulled twisted tight. Miserable old bitch, old b-i-t-c-h, Aunt Bitch, you girls will have to act like young ladies now, but I'll go to the barn if I want to. No braids for me. See the sheep shears, Father's shears hung from a nail on the wall too high to reach, get a stick, big long stick to bring them down, cut it all off, right to the scalp.* Vera watches in the mirror as the girl pulls a comb slowly through the short white hair. The comb stops, meets resistance from a small tangle. The aide very gently begins working on the knotted strands.

Snip. Snip. Brown braids, curled like two small animals on the barn floor. Cat watching from the corner shadows, tail twitching

"Ha ha, old bitch," Vera says, laughing, and the aide, un-certain of the joke, looks relieved when the well-dressed woman with the clipboard in her hand knocks a bit hesitantly on the open door.

"I'll leave you to your visit," she says, and hands the comb to Jeannie on her way out. Vera sits in the dim light of the room, still facing the mirror rather than the door. The curtains are closed; the mechanism that controls them sticks, and Vera hasn't the strength to open them. Jeannie doesn't know this and thinks the old woman must prefer the dark.

"Hello. It's your granddaughter, Jeannie."

Vera doesn't turn from the mirror.

"It's Jeannie. Ian and Elizabeth's daughter." When there is still no answer, she moves into the room and stands beside the chair.

"You look different," Vera says.

Jeannie has not had many conversations with the very old. There is silence as the other woman looks her over, and she finds herself speaking like a country woman, like her mother, words about the weather. "It's a hot day. Are you bothered by the heat?"

"The rooms are air-conditioned. We don't go out much here."

"Of course."

"Where are you staying?"

"The motel on the highway."

"Does it have air conditioning?"

"No."

"It's a long way from Winnipeg."

"Yes. Yes it is. A long drive, especially in the heat."

"Did you take the train?"

"We drove."

"When I was a girl, my sister and I took the train, there was still a station in Eyehill those days, and we went to visit relatives on the Coast. I'll never forget that trip through the mountains."

"I've never been."

In the hallway a uniformed woman walks by, pushing an

empty wheelchair. One of the wheels drags a little, creating an irregular squeak when the rubber catches on the linoleum.

"Dixon will have to fix that," Vera says.

Jeannie feels awkward, as she knew she would, about her reason for the visit. She hasn't had much to do with her grandmother in over thirty years. If she hadn't found the lump, if the specialist hadn't suggested a health history, she wouldn't be here now.

"You might as well sit down," Vera says. "I suppose you're here to talk about your letter."

She is relieved that her grandmother mentions the letter first. She opens her clipboard and takes out a pen to jot down notes.

"Are you married, Jeannie?"

"No."

"I must tell Dixon."

"I'm not married, but I have a friend, a man. He came with me."

"Where is he, then?"

"He's taking photographs." Isaac is working on a series: trees, single, dead trees, standing alone in fields. A metaphor for our own mortality, he'd explained, some tribes believe trees have souls. Trees like these are hard to find. I'll come with you, he'd said, I might see one or two along the way.

"I have some photographs on the dresser. Your father is in the brass frame."

"He doesn't take pictures of people. He wants trees."

"Oh."

"The doctor said to go as far back as possible, two or more generations at least. Do you know anything about your grandmothers on either side?" Jeannie divides the page into four equal-sized columns. Vera looks at the picture of her son and shakes her head about the grandmothers. "What about your mother? Cause of death?"

"Maybe pneumonia. I was only four when she died. Those days people didn't talk of illness with children."

"How old?"

"Thirty-two. After a while, my aunt moved in to look after us."

"Your mother's sister?"

"Yes. Aunt Bess was a school teacher, before she gave it up to raise us. People said she was a saint, looking after her sister's children, sacrificing herself. Before her, we had housekeepers. They came and went every six months or so."

Jeannie writes quickly, without looking up from the page, because she is already behind in her notes, hung up by taking two tries to spell pneumonia.

Who is she, Glorie? A housekeeper, someone who looks after children, a woman with a twisted mouth who does not get dressed until noon, even then spends the day half-fastened, an undone button, a loose shoelace

"How old did you say she was?"

Footsteps in the hallway after I'm in bed, late, late

"Grandmother?"

"Yes?"

"I asked you how old she was."

"Aunt Bess lived a long life, well into her seventies. Never married. Died in her sleep."

Should be sleeping, but I'm scared, there's a woman's voice, a whisper in the dark house that is not mother's, and Father answers it

"Not her. Your mother."

"Thirty-two."

"I wonder why he didn't marry again. A lot of men did."

Father answers it

Vera stares at her hands. Outside, someone starts a lawn-mower. After a moment, she looks straight at Jeannie and asks, "What kind of trees?"

"Trees?"

"Your friend, what kind of trees does he like?"

"Dead ones."

Once again, there is silence between the two women. Then Jeannie asks if she can come tomorrow.

Vera nods. If Jeannie were to look closely, she would see knucklebones, visible and white against the skin of her grandmother's tightly clasped hands. But she is busy writing in the empty spaces of her clipboard: no cancer, no cancer, no cancer.

"Chop some carrots for the soup, will you?" Beryl has already cut the onions, because they bother Noreen's eyes. Wednesday's menu calls for a lunch of vegetable soup and rolls, roast chicken for supper. Beryl is kneading dough.

"How many kids do you have, Beryl? Three?"

"Four. None of them live around here. My youngest boy went to college. He's a landscape designer. Always was crazy about gardens. Used to mow the lawn without being asked."

"What about the others?"

"Mickey's got two boys, but he never sees them. His wife took them with her when she left, on account of his drinking. Roger drives truck. He passes through town once in a while. Theresa is in Ontario, I think."

"You think?"

"That's the last thing she told Roger, and that's all the tight-lipped little bugger would tell me."

Beryl jerks her head in the direction of the counter toward three trays, each set with a small plate, a pot of tea and a cup. "When you're done that, sneak over to rooms two, five and eleven with some toast. Mrs. Adams, Mrs. Powell and Old Scovill didn't make it to breakfast today." The dough slides forward on the counter, moved by Beryl's palms. "I'm happy one of my kids went to college," she says, working the dough until it's smooth. It's taken her years to learn how hard to push, how to shape it just right with her hands.

Man crazy. Slap.

Tramp. Slap.

Who'll have you now? Who?

Alex will. Like a hand held out to a woman who feels the waters closing over her head. A good man who washes after a day in the field, stays sober on a Saturday night. Let's get married, Vera, have a dozen children

"Yes. A dozen."

"A dozen what, Mrs. Powell?" Dixon is fixing the curtain pull in her room. He noticed yesterday when he went by that Vera and her granddaughter sat in semi-darkness.

"Nothing. Nothing much left."

Chin smooth against my shoulder. He shaves more in the winter than another man might, doesn't grow a beard, even for cold, cold days, time spent under the blankets, moving slow because of the weight of sheep's wool comforters, I won't think of music, making an honest place, a place without waltzes, making

"A baby," she whispers.

"What's that?" He bends close to hear Vera's answer. Instead of speaking, she reaches up and lays her hand on his cheek. There is a sound, a soft knocking, and he looks over to see Noreen standing in the doorway. Vera moves her hand away from Dixon and returns it to her lap. He steps back from the chair. Because she is still new to the job, Noreen doesn't know if the touch she just witnessed is against the rules. She does know this: bringing breakfast to the residents in their rooms is not allowed. Her first week, she was told if they miss meals, that's their problem, we can't cater to them. And here she is with a tray in her hands.

He moves away to collect his tools, and Noreen comes in with the food. She takes her time arranging the dishes on the night stand. Dixon leaves, and she waits another minute before going, feeling, for some reason she doesn't understand, that it wouldn't look good for them to be seen leaving the room together.

When Vera opens her eyes, she notices the curtains are pulled back. Sharp sunlight fills the room. She cannot remember missing breakfast and doesn't know why there is a plate of toast by the bed. A bit of present life, the morning hours between waking and the nurse in her room, has been lost. She'd like to ask the nurse if she was sleeping when they brought her pills, but she won't. Say something like that and pretty soon they start to ask questions like, Can you manage the toilet by yourself, dear, or do you want to use the pan? No, she'll just keep quiet, like she does about the times when Alex visits. If she told them about the visits, they'd say, Your husband's dead, Vera, do you need an extra pill to help you sleep? She knows he's dead, but she still sees him now and then, has for months, long before she moved into this place. She worried that grief had put her off her head, but when she told Glorie about it, her sister said, I read something about that very thing the other day. Forty percent of women report seeing their dead husbands frequently. Glorie died too, not long after, but Vera never sees her out of the corner of her eye. Unlike Alex, her sister doesn't cross the line between past and present, except perhaps in dreams.

Last night, she dreamed of trains and, of course, Glorie was there. They were on the way to the Coast. The train rocked along the track, and through the open window it was possible to see the mountains, black and pointed sharp into the night sky. The navy coat. Was it hers? Whose hands spread it on the bed? Difficult to sort, when things that are hidden become tangled with things that are past.

Noreen writes Thursday's menu on the board, drawing a picture of a sheaf of wheat in the space left over. Out of the corner of her right eye, she can see Dixon oiling the hinges of the main entrance doors. Noreen looks for a moment at his profile, the smooth cheek, the hands that hold the door knob. Mrs. Powell is sitting in a chair near the entrance to the dining area. She wonders what the old lady felt when she touched Dixon.

No one has ever said it's wrong, but no one has ever talked about it, either, so there must be something wrong with it, but oh, oh it feels so good, his hand right there. Glorie is the pretty one, but you're the better dancer, he says, and I am, I could dance all night, no one plays "The Tennessee Waltz" like my fiddler does. When you danced with Tom, he says, my eyes never left your sweet

"Good morning, Mrs. Powell," Noreen says. The old lady doesn't answer. She must be having one of her bad days. Doesn't look unhappy, though, just looks past Noreen as if she doesn't see her.

Hand sliding upward. I have on all my clothes, it can't be that wrong, standing close to him outside in the dark shadows of the hall, laughter inside close enough to make us feel we could get caught. Glorie inside, drinking ginger beer with Alex. She's danced three in a row with Alex. I wonder

"What comes next?" the old woman asks.

"It's breakfast time," Noreen explains, "cream of wheat." The old lady touches a hand to her blouse and slides her fingers upwards to the collar, checking the buttons.

"What's wrong with it?"

"Nothing. Nothing's wrong with it. Beryl made it fresh this morning."

"A harmless pleasure?"

"It's good for you."

"Don't be taken in by music," the old woman says.

Noreen goes back to the kitchen and tells Beryl that Mrs. Powell is going downhill fast.

————————

When Jeannie comes, she brings strawberries with her, fresh and sweet. She and Vera eat them outdoors, in the shade of course, but Vera manages to shift out of the darkness so that one shoulder is touched by sunlight.

"I'm afraid some of my questions might be a little personal," Jeannie says, putting another strawberry hull on the little pile they have created on the empty chair seat between them. She sits beside Vera instead of in front of her, so if the questions become embarrassing, they can look at the houses across the street or the caragana hedge that borders the lawn.

"Has anyone in the family ever had . . ." She pauses, unable to go on. At the clinic, she can talk the talk: malignant, benign, metastasize, fibroid, cyst, tumour. Anywhere else, her throat closes on the words.

"Cancer? None that I know of. One of my great uncles had stomach troubles and died young. He might have had cancer."

Jeannie moves on to the next question that her doctor told her to ask. "Did you ever have any problems related to your reproductive system?"

"No. No problems."

"When you were pregnant with my father, was your pregnancy normal? Any complications?" She stops writing in order to look at Vera. Her doctor warned her to be observant, that sometimes older people are unwilling to be completely honest when answering questions about topics that used to be taboo.

"I never felt better in my life than when I was carrying your father. Wasn't sick a day. He was a kicker, always moving, impatient to be born."

"I was the same way, my mother says."

"How is your mother?"

"She keeps busy. Lots of committees."

"She was always very organized."

Jeannie nods, thinking of her tiny childhood dresser, the neat layers of t-shirts resting on lavender paper, the paper changed three times a year.

"A practical woman. She was right to marry again. The year after Ian fell through the ice, I told her no one her age should stay a widow. What about your man friend?"

"He is not very practical. He forgets appointments."

"Has he found any trees yet?"

"No."

"Tell him to drive to Eyehill, take the main road running south of town and go two miles, then turn left at the corner where the Jeffries used to live. There's still an old house there. Tell him to keep driving even when the road grows grass between the tire tracks. He will come to a place where a lake overflowed. All kinds of dead trees. They can't live with their roots in water."

The sudden precision of these instructions unnerves Jeannie, and when she doesn't answer right away, Vera repeats herself. "Did you hear what I said? Water rots their roots. They can't live without a root. Can you remember all that?"

"I'll write it down. I'll tell him."

"I had another child, you know."

"What?" Jeannie is not sure of what she heard.

"Another child. Your father wasn't my first. When he was a baby and I sang to him, I sang for the lost one too. Maybe you need to know that for your history."

Jeannie makes a large question mark on the paper.

"I'm tired now," Vera says, "come back tomorrow. Thank you for the strawberries. Your grandfather used to bring them home for me, picked them wild and put them in his hat."

"Should I get someone to help you inside?"

"No, just leave me here. The air does me good."

The narrow berth in the sleeping car rocks with the movement of the train. Need air. Don't tell Aunt Bess, don't tell father. Keep the sheets clean. Get the blue wool coat. Soak up the blood. Don't tell anyone. Cry quiet so no one will know. Poor little thing. Later, the coat gone, the other gone. Where? Glorie won't say. Where is it buried, the poor dead thing, buried

Later, when Dixon comes around the corner to water the marigolds, the chair is empty, the blanket on the ground, and Vera is kneeling under the trees nearby, hands full of dirt and grass. Dixon picks her up and carries her to her chair. Noreen watches him out the window over the counter. He is strong enough to lift the old woman without stumbling. Back at the motel, Jeannie gives Vera's directions to Isaac, adding, You might get lost, you might never find them. I don't think grandmother's always in her right mind.

"There's going to be a change in the weather, maybe a storm," Beryl says. "I can feel it in my knees." She sits down heavily on a chair by the counter. "Pass me the batter, will you? I'll fill the tins over here." On Fridays, Beryl likes to bake a little treat for the old birds, as she calls them. Her choice this morning is blueberry muffins. Noreen brings the batter and Beryl spoons it in, filling each depression three-quarters full. She dips the spoon without looking at the bowl.

"How do you know what amount to put on the spoon?"

"I can tell by feel, by the weight."

Beryl looks over Noreen's shoulder, says, "You come to fix the stove?"

Dixon, standing in the doorway, nods. "Good thing. I went ahead with the muffins. Knew I could count on you to fix it." She widens her eyes at Noreen, as if to say, See, right under your nose and you don't have the brains God gave you to do something about it.

"Needs a new element." Dixon tries not to look at Noreen in her summer uniform, arms bare and freckled.

"Don't let us hold you up," says Beryl. "You go ahead and peel the eggs for the salad, Noreen. I've got to find some onions in the storage room. I know I ordered twenty pounds just last week." She makes wide eyes at Noreen one more time before leaving the kitchen.

Noreen watches him crouch down to look in the open oven door. His shirt stretches tightly across his back. She taps the egg against the counter and slips the cracked shell away from the cooked white. Her hands become aware of a world of curves, the egg, a man's back, his cheek after he shaves. She runs her fingers lightly over the cool slippery surface of the egg. Dixon's skin would be warm, less smooth, would provide more purchase for her fingertips.

"Another hot day," he says, his head still in the oven. "Weatherman says two more days like this and we'll break the record."

"Beryl says we're due for a change."

"Change'd be good."

Wind in the poplars, leaves turned so the underside faces the sky, a sure sign of rain. Everyone asleep but Glorie, who pretends she doesn't hear me leave the room to meet him. My fiddler's restless before storms, his feet tap a rhythm, his fingers press a sequence of frets into his palm, he stands, he sits, he throws himself onto the soft mossy ground beneath the trees, pulling me down with him. Feel the air, the heaviness, buck against it. Afterwards, he says, I'm leaving.

Vera sits on the closed lid of the toilet seat and ignores the nurse who knocks on the bathroom door.

Too soon. Leaving?

"No."

"Mrs. Powell, don't argue. You have to come out of the bathroom. Your granddaughter is here."

When Vera emerges, the nurse is gone and Jeannie is over by the dresser, looking at the photograph of Ian.

"You look like him," Vera says. "Go on. Take the picture to the mirror in the bathroom. Look at the eyes."

When she comes back, she says, "Not really handsome, but a nice face."

"He was tone deaf, bless his heart. Just like my husband."

Jeannie has questions prepared, but she hesitates because the old lady seems more far-away than usual.

"Glorie was my sister. People said she was the prettiest girl in Eyehill, but I was a better dancer."

"What happened to her?"

"She never said a word about the other baby, and not long after, I married Alex."

"What?"

Vera comes back from the distant place. "Her breasts were fine. It was her heart. She chain-smoked."

"What about you?"

"Smoking isn't among my bad habits. How old are you, Jeannie?"

"Thirty-seven."

"Do miscarriages run in families?"

"I'll ask the doctor."

"What about your friend?"

"He isn't a doctor. He is a photographer."

"I know. Did he find the trees?"

"Yes. He took some pictures."

An excited Isaac had come back to the motel. You should have seen all those trees, he'd said, big ones, small ones. The wind blew through the bare branches, some kind of whisper, a sound without consonants, like the voices of ghosts.

We'll take the train to the Coast. Will we ever be back? she asked, but there was no need, that was the year that everything happened

"Too soon."

"Not at all, Grandmother. He found them just in time. We're leaving tomorrow, going back to Winnipeg."

Vera looks out the window at the blue-black clouds rolling in from the west. "Could I have the photograph?" she says. Jeannie realizes she still has it, that she is balancing it on her clipboard.

"Was your stepfather good to you, Jeannie?"

"Yes."

"Honestly?"

"Yes."

Vera touches a finger to the chest of the young man in the photograph. He is standing in front of a huge woodpile, his axe at rest and a dog at his feet. Jeannie watches her gently rub her thumb back and forth across the glass.

"Glorie said she threw the blue coat off the train."

Jeannie wonders if she should call for a nurse. She goes down on one knee beside the chair and covers the old hand with her own. She feels the delicate, thin skin around the bones, and the cool glass that separates the photograph of her father from the two of them.

"Don't worry. You can always get another coat." No reply. She is learning to recognize the type of silence that signals the end of a conversation. She lifts her hand, straightens and says, "I'll stop on the way out of town tomorrow to say goodbye." Just a short trip to the glass doors, down a hallway. The kitchen must be close by, the air is rich with the smell of roasting meat.

Gravy bubbles on the stove. Beryl is lecturing Noreen on the subjects of Eddie and divorce and children. Noreen says, "I can't see that children give much pleasure. They're a worry."

"True, when they're older, they're a lot of trouble, but when a child's just a baby . . . well, its hard to explain. Don't you think babies are sweet?"

"Sometimes."

"When they're your own, they're always sweet. My mother used to say, Have children, Beryl, and you'll have something for your old age."

Thunder drowns out the cooking noises in the kitchen, big drops of rain pound the roof. Noreen leaves the stove and goes over to the window.

"Look at it come down."

Then she sees the feet, the legs, part of a chair wheel, all exposed to the rain.

"Mrs. Powell," she yells, then runs through the cold-storage room, which has a door that opens onto the driveway. She yells over the storm. "Mrs. Powell, I'm taking you in. It's raining."

The old woman doesn't protest when the chair is turned and pushed towards the door, but she trails her hand behind, as if the chair is a gliding canoe and the rain-filled air is water she lets slip through her fingers. A nurse meets them and takes her back to her room.

When Jeannie arrives to say goodbye, a nurse tells her that Mrs. Powell is probably sleeping, that her grandmother had a little excitement yesterday, so the staff thought it best that she rest. Jeannie goes to the room anyway. Her grandmother is a narrow shape beneath the sheets.

"I'm awake," Vera says, but Jeannie can hardly hear her, just knows that the old woman has made some sound. Vera motions Jeannie closer to the bed, says, "I know what I'm doing, most of the time. They interrupt."

"You are well cared for, Grandmother. The lodge is clean and the food is pretty good. Mother was worried about you."

"Ask me who I married."

"Who did you marry?"

"Alex McNeill."

"Yes."

"Ask me, who is my sister."

"Who is your sister?"

"Gloria Elizabeth Burstall. Ask me, did she want to marry Alex McNeill?"

"Did she?"

"No."

Vera folds the bedspread back a few inches, smoothes it with her hand, feels the blanket, separates it from the sheet beneath it, folds it back, keeping the sheet pulled up for its small warmth. Her fingers sort the layers. *Time for sleeping little baby, good night, sleep tight, don't let the bedbugs bite, oh sweet pea, shh, shh*

"Don't cry," Vera says.

Jeannie does not feel like crying, but there is an impulse, a sudden need to study her grandmother's face, as if it were a map that could lead her to her own urgent desire, newly discovered with the lump. Old age.

"When you get home" — Vera speaks slowly, wanting to be clear — "look at the picture of the trees. Look through them. Up on the hill behind, you'll see a fallen-down house, just the roof rising up through the grass. That was my home when I was a girl. Those trees were . . ." She pauses, seems about to drift off to sleep.

"Grandmother?"

"Sweet pea?"

"The trees?"

The hand moves across the bed sheet until one finger touches the warm spot in the bend of Jeannie's elbow.

"Alive. As we are now."

Lipstick Colours

I left Eyehill on the lope, alone, like one of my Zane Grey heroes, but I'm not a cowboy (or even a man), so I took a job waiting tables at the Athena, a Greek restaurant in Saskatoon. I work the late shift with a woman from Croatia, a refugee who escaped the Communists by crossing the border in the empty belly of a water truck. At least that's what I'm told by the senior waitress who shares our shift. Gordona talks very little about herself. She seems to be everything that life in the city is: foreign, exotic, full of secrets. She does not smile, even for customers.

She's been here longer than I have, so she gets a better section, the wall with the booths by the windows. That's where the new guy always sits. He arrives about ten o'clock, when business is slow. He is tall and thin, with wild, curly hair and crooked eyeglasses. Good-looking in a goofy way, and he knows how to wear his jeans. We have something in common; both of us are fascinated by Gordona.

"In my country," she says, pausing to wipe the table and place a fresh paper placemat in front of him, "the Virgin is called Gospa, which means" — she sets down a knife, a fork, rearranges the fork, then places the spoon; the new guy leans forward, his tongue practically hanging out — "Queen of Peace."

Before he can say anything, she looks at the clock on the wall.

"My break. We have only one, you understand." She nods in my direction. "Rhea will take care of you."

He looks over at me, then down at his menu, disappointed. I pour a glass of ice water, set it in front of him and recite the special. Lasagna, a side of Caesar salad, garlic toast.

Thomas (that's his name, I find out later) doesn't answer, just looks at me with a real intent look, and I'm reminded of my old school bus driver, What Say.

I repeat the words slowly, exaggerating the movement of my lips, just in case he is, in fact, deaf and trying to read them.

"Today, we have . . . lasagna . . . Caesar salad —"

"Did you know," he says, "that the Virgin Mary appeared repeatedly to six villagers on Mount Podbrdo in Yugoslavia?"

I grew up Protestant in a town where all the boys my age could fit into the cab of a truck. One was my cousin, another my friend, and the third was Jarvis (and I didn't kiss him either, though I always thought one day I would). Not much to practise on, not much to use for a comparison, but it's easy to see that Thomas is different from those boys.

"I'd like to have a vision," he says.

I might not have done what I did next if the restaurant had been crowded, but the dinner rush was done and the pub rush was still to come. I'd never done anything like it before, and I might not have done it if it weren't for that night back in early June, when a bunch of us went to the drive-in and I travelled with Jarvis and Carmela and my friend, Roland Lafonde, and they asked Roland and me to go buy some popcorn, and when we came back the windows were fogged, and Roland looked at me and took my arm and said, Let's go eat this in Joseph's truck.

I half-turn so my back is to the rest of the room, lean close to the new guy, looking at him the whole time, my hand moving to the placket of my shirt, my fingers flicking open two more buttons.

"So have one."

His eyes drift down the front of me, up again to my face. I'm not the popcorn girl anymore. It's all there, what you read about, the jolt, and I'm the one who is touching the end of the red wire to the end of the blue wire and making the bell ring.

When my break comes, I take it outside. The cook and the dishwasher watch me slip out the back door. Thomas is waiting beside the Dumpster. He's wearing a loose coat, and because he is skinny, there's a warm space for both of us inside. I feel his chin moving up and down against the top of my head as we pick up where we left off.

"It is said the six still speak with Her, even now, and She reveals to them the secrets of mankind. One moved to Italy, but the visions followed." I nod, recognizing the envy in his voice when he speaks of the six, because I've used that tone myself when speaking of Gordona, so mysterious and so desired.

Joanie Anderson used to draw in ballpoint pen on the bathroom wall: flaming skulls and crossbones, caricatures of our teacher, Mr. Klein, and strangely beautiful pictures of animals with elongated body parts. The janitor scrubbed the wall every night, but she couldn't completely remove the ink, so faint outlines of the drawings remained and, eventually, overlapped. Mr. Klein with his cheeks puffed out like two balloons merged with the eye socket of a skull. A bucking horse arched its back, impossibly long legs stretched into hooves that pointed like the toe shoes of a ballerina.

"You know Joanie Anderson?"

I can tell Thomas is impressed.

"Not very well. She's a fair bit older, but we went to the same school."

"The critics claim she's the next big thing."

Maybe because of Thomas's awe, maybe because of Joanie's drawings, or maybe just because I knew that Carmela would never do such a thing, I decide to take an art class at the university. Thomas picks up the forms I need, I fill them in, pay some money, and here I am, walking to campus for the next to last session.

Thomas is away on a five-day retreat, where there will be ritual purification (a lot of sweating in steam-filled little huts). He's nervous about going because he is a dry-skinned man who doesn't perspire much, and he's afraid of being out-purified by other, more perspirent men. Why the wilderness, I asked, why not the Holiday Inn? They've got a nice little steam room. Apparently, the wilderness is necessary, the insects, the tree roots poking through the ground beneath his sleeping bag, the absence of a woman's back to curl up against. Thomas has been looking forward to it for weeks.

 I walk down Clarence Avenue on my way to campus, past a crew of men filling in a pothole left over from the freeze and thaw of March. It's hot for early May, so this morning I put on a sleeveless shirt. Just sleeveless, not low cut or particularly tight. Just shoulders. But it's enough. One of the men whistles, then another, and a third voice suggests something dirty.

One thing I've noticed about men. How often does a man ever whistle at a woman when it's just the two of them on the street? Never happens. They only do it when there are other men around. The whistling is for the men. It's got nothing to do with me at all.

I like to get to class early, and so does this other woman, Shirley. The two of us sit on the floor on either side of the classroom door and wait. She looks about fifty years old. One day when we were both sitting outside the locked door, Shirley lifted her hands up to her head, palms turned inward like blinkers on a horse's bridle so all she could see was the white wall in front of her (I know because later I tried it myself and that's all I could see), and she says, "I had a daughter about your age, but she's dead."

Another time, Shirley lifted her hands to make the white

tunnel and said, "I didn't raise my daughter. I was sick, you know. I had strange troubles."

The older woman seems to have a lot of problems, one of which is that she cannot draw squares, so she has some difficulty with the chairs. We've spent a fair bit of time drawing sheets draped over chairs (we're Extension, so they won't pay for models for us) and fruit piled up in baskets. The in-structor grits his teeth when she asks him, three and four times, to help her make the chair look right. The concept of parallel lines is lost on her. Last week, the instructor told us to do something at home and bring it to class. He wants to play a game that goes like this: he leaves the room, we tack our papers to the wall, and he tries to guess who painted what.

When I get to the classroom, Shirley's there in the hallway, as usual. I can see only part of her face and her legs from the knees down because the rest of her is behind a huge piece of brown cardboard with the word Maytag printed on it in large red letters. I try the door to see if it's locked, and when it swings open, I hold it for Shirley so she can manoeuvre her way into the room. I can see that the side of the cardboard closest to her body is painted with a face, a woman's face, with a blue shawl draped over the hair. She leans the picture against the wall.

One by one, the other students arrive. The instructor has left a note saying that he is hiding in the supply room, waiting for everyone to put up their work so he can come out.

"Ready yet?" he calls from behind the door.

"Yes," someone says.

I can't take my eyes off Shirley's picture. The woman she has painted wears a robe, the folds in the cloth casting odd dark triangles. The figure is flat-faced, with large eyes positioned too high in a head framed by a slightly flattened halo glittering with gold foil from chocolate bar wrappers and cigarette packages. A mosaic of flowers cut from magazines and wall-paper forms the background. All are surrounded by a shimmering border pieced from foil. The woman's hands are clasped in prayer, but there is no roundness in the shapes; the fingers look like strips of cloth, one woven through the next. They are outlined in dark red, the same red as the lips. The sides of the mouth are twisted unevenly, but I can tell from the posters I've seen hanging in Thomas's apartment that this is the Virgin Mary. First Thomas, now Shirley. It's like going to the mall, trying on a shirt at Reitman's and seeing the same woman that you just saw holding a book in Cole's going into the fitting room next to yours, and then seeing her again later, a few places ahead of you in the donut line.

The instructor steps into the room, looks at the paintings on the wall, then practically runs over to Shirley's, shouting "Whose is this? Who did this?"

She doesn't answer, so I say, "It's Shirley's," ready to defend the shoelace fingers against him, because Shirley can't help the way she sees. The poor woman is half-turned in her chair, looking away from him.

But instead of criticizing, he says, "Marvellous! A masterpiece, a sort of primitive Klimt. Do you know his work?" he asks her.

She shakes her head and says, "But the hands, what about the hands?"

"Wonderfully distorted."

Shirley insists. "The hands don't look right."

He ignores her and asks, "Who is this? Is this who I think it is?"

"Our Lady."

"It doesn't matter who it is," he says, "it's the refreshing naiveté of technique."

"I can't afford paint," she says. "I have strange troubles."

"Wonderfully distorted."

The instructor turns back to the cardboard. He doesn't even notice when Shirley leaves the room. He reaches out to touch the cheek of Our Lady, one finger gently rubbing the surface, trying to figure out what was used to colour the flesh if the artist has no money to buy paint.

Later, I find her in the bathroom by looking under the doors until I see her running shoes.

"It's okay, Shirley. They've all gone home. The instructor dismissed the class early. He had to make a phone call."

"The hands are wrong."

"I know."

"I want them to be right."

"I'll help you with them." I don't know much about portraits, but I figure I can do at least as good a job on the hands as she did. You're too impulsive, Rhea, I can hear Mrs. Bostwick, the Eyehill postmistress, say with her British accent. Then to my father, That girl will get herself into a situation.

We walk to her room at a boarding house just off Twentieth. There is a bed, a small table, a dresser, one chair and a night stand. All the room's surfaces are covered with bottles, jars, crumpled tissues, junk taken from Dumpsters. Very little light gets through the window, which is partially blocked by large sheets of cardboard that lean against the wall beside it. A bottle of glue sits open, the lid lost somewhere. Shirley is anxious to begin. She sets the picture in the best light the room affords.

"What did you use to paint the fingers?"

"Foundation and nail polish, a little lipstick." Shirley waves her hand toward the table and the dresser top, covered with small bottles of nail enamel. Boxes on the floor hold palettes of eye shadow, round compacts of powder, lipstick tubes.

"I think we'll have to start again, make another picture. I'll do the hands first, and you can do the rest later. Okay?"

Shirley nods, lines up various cosmetics and pulls out a fresh sheet of cardboard. The small room is hot and stuffy. Sweat dampens the fabric beneath my arms and make me think of a perspiring Thomas, of the wilderness and green trees, of men's bodies, indistinct pink shapes behind drifts of steam. Shirley has prepared the table. Time to begin.

"I need something to look at, Shirley. Could you sit on the bed and put your hands together, hold them like you want them to look in the picture?" She links her fingers, offers them up in the way of a penitent or beggar. The loose cuffs of her sweater slide down. I start with the fingertips, the triangles that form the spaces between, drawing with a pencil first.

"I don't wear makeup," Shirley says, and it's true. She is a fair-skinned woman with pale lashes, lips barely pink. I draw the fingertips quickly, moving down to the first knuckle. "These cosmetics belonged to my daughter. They cleaned out her apartment after she died, and a man brought the boxes to me. At first, I was happy, you know, to have something of hers, but at night the glass bottles rattled against each other in the boxes. It got so I couldn't sleep. My troubles came back. The woman who owns this place, she took me to the hospital."

The sketch is finished just as her hands begin to shake slightly.

"Are you tired, Shirley? Do you need to rest your arms?"

"No."

"I'm going to start using the colours now."

"Peachfrost is nice," she says.

Peachfrost and Blossomtime for the skin, Terracotta for the shadows where the fingers meet. The colours make me think of Roxanna, who used to babysit me, and the women's magazines she read when I was a kid. The blunt end of the lipstick makes imprecise marks on the brown cardboard. Fingers are difficult. Our textbook says that the old masters, Raphael and the others, who had workshops full of apprentices specially trained to paint sky or fabric or hair, always painted the hands and the faces of their figures themselves. People think fingers are smooth, but they are lumpy, with knuckles just beneath the skin. People think the fingers of their hands differ only in length, but each finger has a shape of its own.

After a time, Shirley speaks again.

"Sandra was my only child. They let me keep her for two

years, even though they suspected the troubles I had, but then they took her. I forgot to change her diaper sometimes. I think that's why."

The tremor in Shirley's hands increases, moves up her arms. I quickly mark a shadow, blend it. Round things don't have hard lines. "She lived with some nice people when I was in the hospital. They told me I could have her back, but when I went to get her, she didn't want to come with me. I took her anyway. She cried. She ran away twice."

Shirley pauses, watching the way the lipstick is stroked onto the cardboard. "How old were you when your mother let you wear makeup?" she asks.

"My mother left my father and me when I was three."

"Sandra always liked makeup. I didn't want her to wear it. Men look at it."

She starts to rock her upper body gently back and forth.

"You can lower your hands now. I can do the rest from memory."

But she stays as she is. The room is warm despite the lack of sunlight, hot enough to make my clothes stick and itch. The bed squeaks the rhythm of the other woman's rocking. Fingers finished, I start working on the ridge of knuckles that separates them from the back of the hand. Shadows cast by knuckles have to be marked subtly. It's the size of the knuckles more than anything that sets a woman's hand apart from a man's.

"See those photographs?" Shirley turns her head toward the wall above the bed. "That's her."

There are pictures taped above the bed, some snapshots, some school photos, one large glossy eight-by-ten. The girl in them looks a bit like Shirley, large-eyed and thin-faced. Short, straight brown hair cut like a boy's in the school pictures, long curly blonde hair in the others. The eight-by-ten is one of those glamour shots, where the studio overdoes the hair and make-up. The background for the shot is flowers. Sandra lies on a flowered sheet, and on top of the printed flowers are scattered real flowers, daisies, roses, tiger lilies. Shirley turns her eyes from the wall. "Men looked at Sandra. She wanted them to. When she was fifteen or so, I knew then. I knew that strange troubles could be passed on to a child."

"Almost finished," I say.

When I was older, my father tried to explain about my mother. Some people are leavers, he said. Some stay put. I paint, ignoring the way the tendons stick out on the backs of the shaking hands, making them smooth and serene, knowing that hands with blue veins and bulging tendons would not look right to Shirley.

"You can lower your arms now." She stops rocking back and forth. The room is quiet, dimmer than ever because the sun is setting and fewer of its rays reach the window. She sits, saying nothing. I sit with her because I don't know what else to do. There is no clock, so I mark time by the darkness of shadows cast by bottles, the diminishing gleams of light reflected by the glass surfaces in the room.

"They said it could have been anyone that did it." Shirley drops her hands, rubs the palms against her legs, pulls down her sleeves. "It could have been another girl, a rival, those kind of girls all carry knives, they said." She gets up slowly, she has been sitting a long time. "It could have been anyone, but I know. I know it was a man."

She goes over to a big black plastic garbage bag in the corner, reaches into it and brings out a handful of paper cuttings. She stuffs them into a small grocery bag, then brings it over and offers it to me. "Thank you," she says. "Thank you for making it right."

I walk home from Twentieth, even though it's a long way, because I want the cool air of evening to blow the heat from my body. By the time I turn the corner onto Clarence Avenue, it's almost dark. Cars come and go, driving over the patches of fresh asphalt left by the crew I'd passed earlier in the day.

What is Thomas doing now?

I imagine him part of a circle of men made pure, sitting around a fire in the night, hands stretched toward the flame. I see their fingers as Shirley would see them, the spaces between lit with orange, outlined by lipstick colours: Summer Melon, Copper Kettle, Terracotta. No amount of sweat removes the stain of that light.

Very Little Blood

Dale always waves goodbye to his children when they get on the school bus in the morning. He doesn't want anyone to know his presence is deliberate (many of his neighbours consider seeing children off to school to be woman's work), so he has to do some planning. When the bus drives in, he arranges to be walking between the barn and the shed, or he stands a little farther away by the corral, holding a hammer and pretending to fix loose boards. In busy seasons, like harvest or seeding, he comes back from the fields when it is time for the bus to arrive because he has forgotten a wrench, a bag of fertilizer, his water jug. Again, he makes sure his son and daughter can see him when he searches for whatever is missing.

The farmyard is large, the buildings within it grouped in a rough circle, creating all sorts of possible paths Dale can walk to be within sight of his children. The barn, old and hip-roofed but still useful, rises from the maze of corral fence around it. South of the barn is a row of granaries. On the rise of ground to the west is the machine shed, most of the farm equipment stored away for the winter. Beside the shed are two broken-down buildings, the remains of a chicken coop and bunkhouse, left over from the days when his mother gathered eggs and his father hired bachelors to work in the summer. The circle is completed by the houses, one an old two-storey, the other a modern bungalow covered with wide strips of vinyl siding, pale yellow, a colour chosen by his wife.

When the kids were young, they always waved back to him. Becky, thirteen, now thinks she is too old to lift a hand in return, but she still looks for him every morning, quick, slight movements of her head showing that she searches for her father by the barn and the fences. His son still waves, but hesitantly, influenced perhaps by seeing his older sister's hands kept low or busy with books and pockets.

The old house is a mottled pigeon grey where the wood has been exposed to weather. It hasn't been painted in years, not since Dale's father died and his mother followed not long after. The plan had always been to pull down the old house once the new one was finished. He'd built the bungalow for his wife before they married because she wanted it and he could afford it. The two houses are separated by no more than the space of a driveway. The front door of the old house faces the narrow side of the bungalow's rectangle, casting a long shadow that prevents his wife from growing flowers there. The day he'd moved back into the old house, his wife pulled the blinds on the windows he might have looked into from his dead parents' porch, stretching the shadow, pulling the darkness inside.

He knows everyone in Eyehill is talking about how Dale Jewison's wife cheats on him with Lenny Morris. How the two of them sleep together right in Dale's own yard, in the house he built for her. How he puts up with it. "A real man . . ." they'll be saying in the coffee shop. "A real man wouldn't . . ." or "A real man would . . ." When the affair between his wife and Morris first became known, Eyehill had been on Dale's side, but he can feel that changing. He's seen how it works. Take sports, for example. When the home team doesn't make the playoffs, no one stops watching. They pick another team, and this time they try to pick a winner.

At first, Morris's business suffered. He runs a makeshift shop out of Jerry Daniel's machine shed from April through November. The rest of the year, he works as a mechanic in some mine up north. When talk of the cheating was fresh, farmers who knew Dale wouldn't take their tractors to Morris. They drove the extra miles to Airedale, but he hears that these days Morris isn't short of work. He's a good mechanic. It was Jerry who first hinted that Dale's wife might be fooling around with Lenny. "Having equipment trouble this spring?" he'd asked. "Saw your wife over at the shed three times last week."

Only two of the neighbours had guts enough to bring the whole bad business up with him face to face. Roy Lafonde said, "Why don't you rent the land? Get the hell out for a while. You look terrible. I got a cousin in BC can get you work logging for the winter." Dale thanked him for coming and turned down the offer. Skipper Jake said, "Get a lawyer and run her off the place." He nodded to show that he had heard.

Last month, Dale travelled to the city to see a doctor. A specialist. He has a rash on his legs. It burns and itches and his pants rub him raw. The doctor's office was in a busy part of the downtown. In the few blocks from where he'd parked his truck to the door of the clinic, he walked past more than twenty men. All those men might have unfaithful wives, every one of them, but no one on that street knew it. What freedom, Dale thought, what a relief. The doctor could not name the rash. Might be stress, he said, try to relax more. Find a hobby where you can work with your hands.

Dale thinks of his parents often, now that he is living alone in the old house. The rooms bear the stamp of their habits. There are hooks on the wall in the porch where his father hung the layers of heavy clothes he wore in the winter months. His father took off his gloves first, laid his hat aside on the chair by the door, hung his coat on a peg, then retrieved the hat and hung it on the peg above the coat. Boots were unlaced last, the right and then the left. The wooden table still stands by the kitchen sink where Dale's mother sorted wet laundry and hung it on the line in groups, button shirts, then short-sleeved white undershirts, then pants.

He watched his parents at their rituals. The way his mother set the table for breakfast the night before, teacups on saucers for the adults, a glass for Dale's milk, three bread plates and bowls for cereal. His father sat at his left, his mother at his right. His father arrived home for meals at twelve noon and six p.m. no matter what the season. He was the only farmer in Eyehill who left the field at harvest to go home to eat. Sometimes he was a few minutes early, but he was never late.

He sees now that such patterns were deliberate, each domestic detail piled one on top of the other like straw bales in a stack. It had started when he was very young, the summer before he went to school. It was Sunday night and there was nothing good on TV. He remembers the table set with dishes, the light in the room growing less and less, the movement of his mother's hand as she pulled back a curtain to look out the window, pulled it back again and again even after it grew dark, and there was nothing to be seen. His mother gave him half slices of bread and butter to dull his hunger as they waited for his father, who might come home at any minute, but who never came at all that night.

Dale stayed in bed as long as he could the next morning, but the time came when he had to go to the bathroom, and going to the bathroom meant walking by the doorway to the kitchen. He had walked on tiptoe, not wanting to be noticed, and as he passed the kitchen doorway, he saw his mother putting away the unused cutlery from the night before, wiping each fork, knife and spoon with a tea towel even though they were clean and dry. Now and then she pressed the folded edge of the tea towel to the corners of her eyes.

The cupboard drawers were empty when he moved back into the old house. There are dark patches on the walls where his mother hung pictures of Pinkie and Blue Boy, marks on the

kitchen floor where the wood stove used to be. But he is working on filling these empty spaces. Now there are enough dishes
in the cupboards for him and the kids to use. They eat with
him three times a week, and he serves anything they like that
comes in a can or he scrambles eggs. There is always ice cream
in the freezer. Dale has a television, a rack for his magazines.
He sleeps on a mattress on the floor of his old bedroom. When
he climbs the stairs at night, he can feel the uneven surface of
the sixth step through the thickness of his socks, the wood
notched with several shallow cuts.

When Dale looked through the door and saw his mother
crying, he'd been filled by the certainty that his father was
never coming back. His father. Gone. When his mother went
out to gather eggs, he went to the wood box, where his father
kept the hatchet. He took the leather cover off the blade. If his
father had been there, Dale would not have been allowed to
touch the hatchet, but his father was gone. He carried the
hatchet to the stairs, and chopped at one of the steps. He went
to the kitchen, lifted the blade high above his head and buried
it in the seat of his father's wooden chair.

A few days later, he woke up in the morning and heard his
father speaking to their dog in the odd, high-pitched tone he
reserved for animals. The sound drifted into his room through
the screen of a half-open window. Dale does not remember any
arguing, any raised voices in the night. No explanation was
offered. He watched his father smooth away the worst of the
hatchet marks in the wood of the stairs, and he tried to collect
the fragile shavings in his palms as they curled up in front of the
plane. The more he thinks about it now, the more certain it
seems that the habits of the old house date from that time.
Dale's parents did not believe in anger. His father did not bang
his fist on the table talking politics with the neighbours. His
mother wiped muddy footprints off her freshly scrubbed floors
without comment. It was a quiet house. Every room had a
ticking clock.

He spends a lot of time trying not to picture his wife in bed with Lenny Morris. The trouble is, his wife's body is all too easy for him to imagine. It's more difficult to think of Morris without clothes, so when he pictures his wife and a naked man together, the man's body is always Dale's own. His own naked legs, long back and almost hairless chest. The scar just below his armpit where a steer ran him into a barbed wire fence. It is Dale's bones that show through the naked man's skin, but when the man rolls over onto his back, he sees that the face belongs to Morris.

His wife hadn't even tried to lie. "Lenny and I had a thing going in high school," she said. "It never really stopped."

When Dale courted her, he took his time, made sure she saw him at least twice a week, no fast moves. She worked at the Eyehill Café, so he went in for coffee more often, not late in the morning, when it was busy, but around nine o'clock, when sometimes there was no one else in there but him and her and the owner, who lived in the back and watched television, coming out only when he had to cook. He talked to her about the weather, then more personal things: her favourite songs, where she went shopping, the bad repair job her landlord had made of the bathroom faucets. Then he asked her on a date and she said yes. When he took her home, he hadn't tried anything, and she'd been surprised but pleased. She said later that she'd felt as if he was taking her seriously, as if he wanted more from her than just ten minutes in a truck cab, when half a man's attention was on trying not to get hung up on the gear shift.

From the very first time Dale made love with his wife, he was methodical. He knew there were a few men who'd been there before him, better men, maybe, and he was afraid. He took off her shirt first, kissed the palm of her right hand, then her wrist, the bend of her elbow, her shoulder. Did the same thing with the left arm. She undid her bra, and lay back on the bed while he knelt over her, placing a hand on each breast. He worked his way over every surface of her body, marking a path to follow the next time and the next. When she became pregnant with Becky, he learned the new largeness of her so well that when a nurse handed him his baby daughter, he felt he already knew the shape and weight of the child in his arms. His wife said she liked the fact that he didn't hurry. When it came to the act itself, he tried to think of other things, calculating bushels per acre on crops he had seeded or the tax on a new tractor, forcing himself to count, twenty-three, twenty-four. Twenty-five seemed like enough.

And it was, for a while, but looking back, he can see that his wife grew bored. She went to town four days a week instead of once or twice, returning to the Eyehill Café, a customer now who sat for entire afternoons drinking coffee and smoking, the chair on the other side of the table sometimes empty, sometimes occupied. Morris must have sat with her some of those afternoons, watching the movement of her lips as she talked, both of them remembering what it had been like in high school.

Keeping his hands busy helps to ward off images of his naked wife. He builds an addition to the corral, measures each board twice, cuts them to exactly the same length, even if it means measuring again, shaving a thin wafer of wood off the end. Sometimes it works, and the only thing he feels is the prickle and itch of the rash on his legs when he starts to sweat. Sometimes it doesn't, and those times the smooth shape of the saw handle is his wife's hip bone, the rasp of the blade on wood her quickened breath. The heads of the nails are Lenny Morris, and he splinters the boards each time his hammer falls.

He remembers Becky learning to crawl, not getting the hang of moving one knee forward, then the other. She'd drag herself along with her hands, finally collapsing on the floor in a fit of giggles or rage. He'd knelt down with her and guided her small, fat legs with his hands, moving one bent knee forward at a time. Once she'd learned to crawl, caution made her slow to walk. She didn't want to let go, clinging to the things she was sure of: the edges of chairs, the crib railing, his wife's hands, his hands.

Not long ago, he saw that his wife had hung more than the usual amount of laundry out to dry. The sight of so many clothes twisted Dale's gut. What if they were being washed so they could be packed in suitcases? What if his wife decides to go up north with Morris and takes the children with her? Surely she would tell him? Maybe not. The strange equilibrium of their households depends on each one pretending the other is not in the yard. He knows his wife wishes him gone. One day he saw her walking toward the old house with a gas can in her hand. She's going to burn it, he thought, burn me out. It had only been the lawnmower, the tank empty and needing fuel, but he is sure his wife sometimes dreams of fire.

His daughter is eating supper with him. Greg is away at a birthday party for one of his friends. Dale didn't realize before tonight how much he depends on his son for conversation. Greg doesn't guard the details of his life, talks about school and friends and hockey teams. All Dale has to do to communicate with Greg is watch a few hours of television in the evening, and then the two of them can talk for as long as they choose about what people on the various shows are doing. Greg loves to retell the plots of sitcoms and laugh again at the jokes. Becky picks the mushrooms off her pizza and says nothing.

"What are you thinking, Becky?" A question born of desperation, a silly question he's never asked before.

Becky pauses for a minute. He hopes she will say she is thinking of nothing and the two of them can go back to the desperate quiet, but she says, "I'm thinking how I'd like to change my name."

"What's wrong with Becky?" As soon as he says the words, he realizes that Becky is a little girl's name, so he corrects himself. "What's wrong with Rebecca?"

"Nothing," she says. "It's not my first name I want to change. She's talking about changing hers. After the divorce. She wants her maiden name. Then my name will be different from hers." Becky is playing with her fork and knife as she speaks. He watches her slide the knife blade through the tines and use it as a lever to bend the metal of the fork. "And I'll be glad," his daughter says, working steadily to destroy the fork. "I'll be so fucking glad."

"Nothing's been decided about a divorce," he says, feeling the tingling itch snaking up and down his legs. Becky's never used such language before. The rash wants to be scratched. Dale wants to scratch out the sound of his daughter's grown-up curses.

"You both make me sick," she says. "Do you know what they say about you at school? What I have to pretend not to hear them saying? Why don't you do something?"

"What?"

"Hit him," his daughter says. "Beat him up. Kick him out. Be a man."

He rubs his palm over the fabric that covers his thigh. Becky is so angry. He looks over to where the wood stove used to be. The hatchet has been gone for years. A good thing maybe, because if it were there, he would take the leather cover off with his own hands, give the sharp blade to his daughter and say, go ahead, with all your might.

"But you won't," she says. "You won't do anything." And she leaves the table, runs back to the dubious refuge of the yellow house.

No sleep that night. It is the first time he's passed an entire night without even closing his eyes. He sits in a chair in the

living room without lights. He has worked hard to keep his
children safe from violence. Take the calves, for instance. Sometimes calves are born with something wrong with them. They
lie on the floor of the barn, unable to drink, unable to stand,
bawling steadily, as if something unseen hurts them. Calves
such as these all die after two or three days of suffering. He
knows from experience there is no cure, but he waits until late
at night to shoot them. He loads the calves into the back of the
truck and takes them away from the yard before he pulls the
trigger so Becky and Greg won't hear the shot. He has never
raised a hand to his children. Never even raised his voice.

His eyes have grown so accustomed to the dark room that
he can see the ridged tendons on the backs of his hands. Even
small details, like the fine stripe in the wallpaper, have become
visible. If he were to hit Lenny Morris, he would prefer the fight
to be like something from an old movie, a few decisive blows to
the face, perhaps one to the stomach that would lift the other
man right off his feet. Morris would fall. It would end with
very little blood.

A thin, bright line marks the horizon. Maple trees his parents
planted to shelter the yard rise black against the sky. He tightens the lug nuts on the tires of the swather, preparing to put
the machine away for the winter. Lenny Morris's truck is parked
in the driveway. He has started spending nights, but he leaves
in the morning before the bus arrives, perhaps trying to avoid
any talk the bus driver might start around town. Dale pulls
upward on the tire iron, feeling the strength he needs to turn
the nut moving from the soles of his feet up through his body
to his shoulder. He expects Morris to come outside anytime
now, and he wants to be ready, so he works by touch in the
semi-darkness, never taking his eyes off the house.

Not long after he started living apart from his wife, a minister came to see him. A stranger, a man Dale had never seen

before, sent to him by some well-meaning neighbour who was part of a faith stronger than his own.

"The Lord tests us," he said. "Abraham. Isaac. Forty days in the wilderness. Old Testament, New Testament, one test after another."

Kneeling beside the swather, his legs stinging where blood from the raw patches of his rash has soaked into his long underwear and made it stick to his skin, Dale thinks of the minister's words. A test. Waiting for Lenny Morris to come out.

A few minutes later, when Morris does emerge, he is in a hurry, walking fast, eyes straight ahead, careful not to look anywhere Dale might be. The bus is coming, a faint engine noise from far away. Morris walks by the passenger side of his truck, stops, goes back a few steps and bends down, disappears from sight for a minute. Then he pops up, searches the back of the truck, doesn't find what he is looking for, and walks back to the house.

Dale knows what the problem is. Morris has a flat tire and no tools to change it. The tire iron that should be in the back of the truck is gone.

It isn't long before Morris comes out again, this time with Dale's wife, who stands in her bathrobe on the wooden step and points toward the shed, telling Morris where to find the tools he needs to fix the tire. Dale sees all this from his place behind the swather. Morris starts walking toward the building, and the closer he gets, the larger he looks, his body blocking Dale's view of the door where Becky and Greg will soon appear.

Dale planned every step of the confrontation with Becky's words, *fucking glad*, echoing in his mind. He imagines raising the tire iron, bringing it down as hard as he can, the crack of ribs, the froth of a punctured lung, broken teeth. He sees it all clearly. Once Morris goes down, he'll stop hitting him.

The bus drives in the yard, its headlights shining on the swather blades. When he hears the door of the yellow house slam behind his children, Dale straightens up from where he crouches in the shadow cast by the bulk of the machine. Morris stops less than six feet away, his face surprised and wary. He did not expect Dale, did not expect the tire iron. The bus driver stares, and all the kids inside have their noses pressed to the windows.

Morris stands perfectly still. Maybe he is afraid to move. Maybe he is judging the distance between them, calculating his risks. Becky will be watching. Dale half-raises the iron and takes a slow step forward. She'd said he wouldn't do anything. I know you won't do anything, she said. So sure of her father.

When he tells the story later that morning, Morris will not admit to the fear he felt when he faced Dale Jewison. Crazy bastard, he'll say, shaking his head and trying for a laugh. Handed me the iron. Just handed it to me, like I'd said please.

Do as I Do

"This is where they found him," says the woman hired by the lawyer to look after the house, "in his undershorts, his head lying on the mat in the hall. Taken by a heart attack." Her hand hovers close to the pocket of her stretch pants, ready to offer a Kleenex from the wad that bulges there, waiting for a response. Joanie steps further into the room and runs her hand along a windowsill.

"Do you think this is oak?" she asks.

Phyllis has prepared answers for other kinds of questions. No, dear, your grandfather didn't suffer. Quick and painless, the doctor said. However, she rises to the occasion.

"Not likely. Too fine a grain. Maple, maybe, or birch."

Joanie nods. One of the few things she remembers fondly about this rigid house is the trim around the doors and windows, the chair-rail, the pattern made by the grain of wood. The windows are large and multi-paned, opening the room to the rich, orange light of an early summer sun sunk close to the horizon.

La fenêtre. Joanie thinks of the window in French. Her grandfather taught her how to say it properly, so that the last syllable rhymed with wet, not with etcetera, which was incorrect but the only way her grade seven French teacher, who was also the math teacher and the health teacher, knew how to pronounce it. A whole generation of children left the Eyehill school and enrolled in French classes in Airedale thinking that *chat* rhymed with hat. She had sat here in the living room in the blue chair, with her copy of *Douze Contes Faciles*, and the old man, who'd picked up the language during the war, taught her to speak French with a Paris accent.

Les mots, she said, rhyming it with dots.

No, no, he would stop her, like this. Then he'd purse his lips, and sounds that were incomplete for the letters emerged: *les mots*. Like doe or hoe. While she learned the importance of silent letters, her grandmother, a woman of miserly habits, played solitaire in the kitchen with a deck so old the intricate blue pattern on the back of each card was worn away at the corners.

"Delivered a week ago," Phyllis says, pointing to the mattress, still wrapped in plastic, propped up against the living room wall. They pass into the kitchen. Joanie opens a cupboard door. Someone has carelessly wiped the shelves, leaving behind rough patches where spilled sugar still clings to the surfaces.

"We cleared everything out last year," she says, watching Joanie's fingers come away from the shelf. "I used my own judgment about what wasn't worth keeping. That's what the lawyer said to do."

Joanie nods.

"One more thing."

Phyllis takes her upstairs, into her grandfather's bedroom. His dresser, four large drawers with a row of six smaller drawers up one side, still stands against the wall. Each drawer has a keyhole.

"We didn't want to sell this." She tugs on the brass handle of one of the small drawers. "On account of it being locked. We couldn't find the key."

Joanie nods, thinking of how her grandmother used to keep money in a jewellery case, of how she'd learned to pick that lock, take what she wanted, and never leave a mark on the silver fitting.

"I'll be all right now," Joanie says, "on my own."

Still an odd girl, Phyllis will tell her husband when she gets home. A cold girl.

Joanie inserts a bobby pin into the keyhole of the drawer and wiggles it, listening for clicks in the mechanism. Her talents (picking locks is one) are born of dishonesty. She learned to draw by copying her grandfather's signature on discipline notes the teachers sent home from school. He had been supposed to sign them as proof that he'd been informed of her unwise decisions. "Dear Guardian, We regret that Joan has, for the second time this week, been involved in hostile encounters with . . ." It was not difficult to imitate his handwriting, so she tried copying other things, the figure of the queen of diamonds, a greeting card, the cereal box. When this became too easy, she copied the movements of cats that walked the fence rails.

She pulls on the handle, maintaining a gentle outward pressure, wiggles the pin again, and the drawer slides open. Inside is a shallow box, the lid carved with random, sinuous lines. Something about the colour of the wood and the nature of the carving makes her think of Africa.

There are postcards inside. Images on thick paper, the edges yellowed. She shuffles through them, counts twenty-seven. The pictures are all of one woman in various stages of undress. Background and props change, but the cigarette is constant, an awkward *S* of hand-painted smoke rising from its tip.

The one on the top shows the woman wearing black garters, a chemise sliding from her shoulder. Her lips are slightly parted, ready to receive the cigarette. Joanie turns the image over.

1918, written in the top corner, in lines of black ink as fine as spider silk.

The message: *I do not care what the photographer sees, because I can tell he is in love with his machine, his magic camera eye.*

The signature: *Dolores.*

The photograph could be one frame of a silent film, a melodrama in which the heroine will soon be hoodwinked by the villain and tied to the railroad tracks. It could be, but Joanie sees there is nothing naive in the angle of the cigarette. If there is a train coming, this half-dressed Dolores knew it all along.

Joanie unloads her car: an overnight bag, a cardboard box of food, two wooden crates filled with rags and brushes and tubes of paint, bought from a man whose business card reads Maurice Jones, Fine Art Supplies. The city where she lives is small, can support only one store of this kind, and Maurice also sells model airplane kits and glue guns and pipe cleaners.

It is night enough for the bright star near the horizon to show itself, but not quite dark. She sheds her clothes in the privacy of the windowless hall (all the curtains have been sold) and puts on a swimsuit several decades old, purchased at a thrift shop. The fabric is thick and scratchy and indestructible, capable of absorbing three times its weight in water.

She slips out the door and walks through the back yard, an overgrown acre of wild roses surrounded by a shelterbelt of spruce, the leg openings of the swimsuit rubbing low on her thighs. Closer to the house, her grandmother's peonies have shed their petals in patterns of white beneath the pointed leaves. Beyond the line of spruce, there is a slow-moving creek fed by springs. Years ago, some trick of its bending created a small, deep pool. Willows grow along the bank, cattails and a few poplar trees, green things that smell sweetest at dusk.

Three steps from the soft mud of the creek bank and she is chest-deep in water. She takes a breath and sinks below the surface, her favourite part of immersion, when the weight of her hair is lifted. It floats above her, and the slightest turn of her head sends it twisting. She surfaces to breathe, then bobs slowly in the dark, delicious coldness. One of the swimsuit's wide straps slips off her shoulder. Her heart beats faster. She reaches for the other strap. Such a tingle. She takes a deep breath and submerges completely. Lift the knees, make the body a loose ball floating. Strip the swimsuit down past waist, past hips. Ignore the need to breathe. The suit tangles momentarily at the ankles, then it is off. Her feet find the bottom and she comes up for air. Her head is visible, nothing more. She glances down and then quickly away from the sight of her breasts, two white smudges, like fingertip marks of chalk on the dark background of water.

She'd lived for a time with two women. Both owned full-length mirrors and stood before them regularly, observing their bodies, comparing the cleavage created by this bra or that, turning round to check the drape of a skirt. One frequently pinched the skin of her waist and pencil-tested the curve where buttock met leg. If there was flesh enough to trap a pencil there, she skipped breakfast for a week. The other took hot baths and afterward stroked scented oil into her skin, massaging legs and arms, hips and belly. The woman who stroked herself used to print the telephone numbers of therapists on the backs of envelopes, dropping them like hints throughout the apartment.

Music, the sound of fiddle and guitar, faint in the cool air above the creek. A party for someone at the Eyehill Community Hall. Neck deep, the water touches Joanie everywhere, cool and smooth and hairless, a clean embrace without heat or sweat.

Want.

Rising in her like the smell of cellar damp through a floor-board crack.

He watches her pick up a paint brush and rub her thumb over the soft sable bristles. She wants to ask him a question. Why is the name Maurice followed by Jones? Is Maurice a pseudonym, adopted because it sounds French and therefore arty?

"I'd never make any money if every one of my customers were like you," he says.

Joanie pretends not to hear.

"All you ever buy is black."

He follows her around a corner.

"Black is the cheapest paint I carry. What about a tube of alizarin at twice the price? Or a nice cobalt blue?"

He selects a large tube from the shelf beside him and turns toward a piece of white paper, tacked to the wall, daubed with dots and squiggles of many colours. He squeezes a bright bead of paint onto his fingertip and lets the finger smear the paper slowly, leaving a lazy snake trail of hot pink.

She presses the pointed wooden end of the brush into her palm.

"Is Maurice your real name?"

He picks up a rag to wipe his hand. "My mother is a hockey fan," he says, "Montreal is her favourite team."

The phone rings — once, twice, three times — and he turns away to answer it. She watches the back of his head, tilted to trap the phone between his ear and shoulder, and the movement of his arm as he picks up the clipboard and writes something across a page, doing it all without clumsiness or hesitation.

She reads sections of newspapers that others have left behind on bus seats and park benches. Not long ago, she saw a study that claimed nearly twenty percent of alcoholics give up drinking without formal rehabilitation.

Maurice wears a t-shirt, and the skin of his arms is smooth.

Not even a twelve-step program. No formal rehabilitation of any kind.

He laughs into the telephone.

She doesn't like the taste of alcohol, has never been at risk that way, but the numbers stay with her. One-fifth, the study said. One-fifth have the power to heal themselves.

———————

Suzy. Standing on the doorstep, her hairstyle unchanged since high school: long and straight, with bangs rolled back by a curling iron. She smiles when she sees Joanie peeking from behind the makeshift curtain. Her sweatshirt is stretched tight across her breasts and pregnant belly. She carries a bag of Cheezies in each hand.

"I heard through the grapevine you were here. Down at the store, Phyllis is telling everybody not to worry if they see lights burning at the old Daniels place." She steps inside and raises her arms slightly, the beginning of a hug, perhaps, then stops. She offers Joanie one of the bags. She looks at the mattress on the floor, the bolt of canvas in the corner, the fabric unwound from it, the same cloth used to cover the windows.

"Just like camping. Like the night we all slept on the ground, out behind Winston's father's barn."

"I don't remember," Joanie says. "Maybe I wasn't there."

"I must be thinking of another time." Suzy moves over to the mattress. "Mind if I sit?" She drops down cross-legged and opens her bag of Cheezies. "I really shouldn't. The doctor says I have to eat better with this baby, but he doesn't know what it is to be a pregnant woman. The cravings. Days when I'm waitressing at the café, if no one's looking, I'll lick my finger and dip it right into the salt shaker."

Joanie moves her sketchbook off one of the boxes and sits on it, facing her. Suzy looks down at the closed cover, at the scattering of pencils on the floor.

"Phyllis says you're an artist." She pops another Cheezie into her mouth, then rolls her eyes. "Pardon me, she says you *call* yourself an artist."

That eye roll. The gesture flattens time; something in Joanie heaves, then settles warmly into place. This is Suzy, her friend since they were thirteen. She flips the sketchbook open. A drawing of Dolores, all curves and muslin ruffles. A note jotted beneath, copied from the message on the postcard. *Do. As I do.*

Her friend looks down at the drawing. "You're better than ever."

"What I remember," Joanie says, "is the summer we robbed the Molson truck."

Suzy giggles. "I've had a weakness for truckers ever since."

Joanie had lifted the cases out of the truck after Suzy led the driver, a guy not much older than they were, into the little shed behind the hotel. Later, they sold the beer cheap to the guys on the ball team who practiced in the field by the rink.

Suzy brushes some crumbs from her protruding stomach. "What was it we were going to use the money for?"

"Bus fare."

Suzy takes another handful of Cheezies. "What about you? You got a boyfriend?"

"No."

"Phyllis says the house is going to be for sale."

Joanie nods.

"Phyllis says she doesn't understand how the old man's will could leave out Jerry. She wants to know how come you get the house, when the old man's own son is still living right here in Eyehill."

"I never asked for any of it."

"What's it to you, Phyllis? That's what I asked her." Suzy rolls down the top of the half-empty bag of Cheezies and shifts her weight, preparing to stand. "Old bat's always had a soft spot for him. Never mind that she's married." She looks sideways at Joanie. "We both know a woman like Phyllis is way too old to interest your Uncle Jerry."

Joanie offers a hand to help her up.

"Does he know you're here?" Suzy asks.

"If you know, then he knows."

Later, Suzy tells anyone who asks that Joanie is doing well. Never mind that Joanie doesn't wear makeup or wash her hair very often, that she wears clothes that were obviously sewn for a much larger, much older woman. She looks good, is what

Suzy says. And her career? Well, she's on her way to being famous.

Joanie's most recent exhibition is a series: black canvases, each with an indistinct figure, a few brush strokes of pale green, painted like a tiny flicker of light in the top left corner. A process her grade six teacher taught her. Cover paper with crayon colours. Cover the colours with India ink so all seems black. Take a small, sharp object, an uncoiled paper clip, a pin or a pencil lead, and scrape away the black to reveal the rainbows underneath.

If only they had known, the men and women who looked at the paintings, those who finally bought them, they could have taken a coin or fingernail and scraped off the top layer of black to expose another picture: a row house with a narrow back yard, a plum tree, a concrete swan (its back hollowed and filled with geraniums), a cocker spaniel asleep in the shade of a long white car, a small girl on a swing, her father in front, his arms lifted to catch her, her mother behind.

The adults are going on a trip without the child.

She is going to stay in the country for a short time, a week and two days, just a *short* time, with the grandparents and the mother's much younger brother. Uncle Jerry keeps horses.

The train goes off the tracks.

The house, the tree, the swan, the car — sold in a quick and poorly advertised auction, while the girl is packed into a trunk.

No. Her things are packed.

The dog? She never had a dog, but she wanted one.

Her mother's old bedroom, newly wallpapered with tiny blue flowers and still smelling of the paste. The girl is too short. She cannot reach.

A plastic figure dangles from the light string, a boy wearing pointed clogs.

Her grandmother must come in to pull the string that turns

out the light. Wednesday nights, she has church business. Don't
worry.

Uncle Jerry will see to it.

The critics are delighted with the paintings, with Joanie's
slim flickers of light. Spirit creatures, said one. Ethereal brush
strokes, said another. They could not, after all, have known
about the Dutch boy, swaying, glowing like the hands of the
watch on Uncle Jerry's wrist. An eerie green form tied there
specially to be a comfort to children in the dark.

Dolores wears a pair of pants, cinched high and tight at the
waist. The ends of a scarf fall between her bare breasts, a flat cap
rests on her head. Dolores wears a negligee trimmed in ostrich,
sits curled up in a chair by a table with a jar of peacock feathers,
wears ostrich-feathered mules. The pose is modest, her stock-
inged legs drawn up and crossed, her negligee tied loosely.

Joanie turns the second picture over and neatly prints a tiny
number in the top right-hand corner, in the place where there
would usually be a stamp. The postcards, their messages puz-
zling and incomplete, must have been hand-delivered. They
smell of something antiseptic, an odour absorbed from the
exotic wood of the box.

Trainloads of wives are returning to Paris.

Joanie tries to imagine what it is in these pictures that might
excite a man. Dolores is seldom in the bedroom. Usually she sits
on a parlour chair or reclines on a couch, surrounded by cushions. Perhaps it is the thighs, smooth and broad, Dolores con-
torted to best display the inner surface of the leg furthest from
the camera. One breast is bared more often than both. Joanie
examines and numbers each postcard methodically. If an image
doesn't appeal to her, she turns the card face down. In the end,
she is left with three: Dolores in pants, Dolores in profile
blowing smoke toward the ceiling, and her favourite, the one
she finally chooses, setting the other two aside. Dolores looking

straight at the camera, the negligee parted so her breast peeks out from behind the ostrich feathers, an elegant tilt to her wrist as she holds the cigarette. Words on the back. *What do I fear? Not the ground rising up to meet me. No. It's that small pain a woman on a trapeze must feel each time her partner catches her, that regular, anticipated wrench of shoulders in their sockets.*

A yellowed gap, an expanse of paper, before the command that ends the message.

Do not ask me again.

A knock on the door. Joanie gathers the cards into the box, flips the corner of a blanket over it, and goes to answer it. The man standing outside is a stranger. On the street behind him, a cube van idles.

"You the one ordered the chaise lounge?" he asks.

All of the windows but one are covered by closed curtains. Joanie's doors are locked. The uncovered window is large and divided into many small, square panes. This morning, she sank the feet of a stepladder into the soft grass of the lawn, climbed high enough to reach the top panes of glass, and, working her way down, brushed the outside surface of every pane with black paint. Then she went inside and started hammering together two-by-eights and sheets of heavy plywood, creating a slightly raised platform about six feet square.

Tonight, she lifts the chaise longue into position on the platform, which is directly across from the window. One of the cushions is placed against the back and the other two are allowed to fall to the floor behind it. Occasionally, Joanie glances at the postcard for guidance. The small table, surprisingly heavy to carry, is set slightly in front of one of the arms of the chaise longue. She takes a package of cigarettes from the breast pocket of her shirt, removes the cellophane wrap, extracts one of the cigarettes and places it on the table.

The same grade six teacher who'd taught her about wax

crayon and ink and scraping also taught her how to use a grid. She remembers struggling to copy a picture of a spotted lily from a garden catalogue. Her teacher took a pencil and a ruler and, with swift precision, divided the lily into many small squares. Then he divided the drawing paper into an equal number of larger squares and explained. Copy the lines and shapes into the large squares, exactly as they appear in the smaller ones, and the whole is duplicated. A particular problem, like the deep, freckled throat of the lily, can be solved by geometry. The window panes — painted black outside and left untouched inside — now act like mirrors, reflecting the furniture. The narrow bands of wood between the panes are grid lines, dividing the furniture arrangement into squares.

She sets the postcard on the table beside the cigarette. Faint pencil lines divide the image of Dolores into parts. Joanie unbuttons her shirt, sits, checks her position, wiggles a little closer to the raised back of the chaise longue so she can rest an elbow on its upholstered surface. She picks up the cigarette, studies the section of the postcard containing the hand and, guided by the window grid, imitates the languid bend of Dolores's wrist as she allows the cigarette to droop between her index and middle fingers. Her body relaxes, slanting toward the back of the chaise where her elbow supports her torso. The postcard and the reflection match from the waist up.

Now the legs. Allow one to dangle from the edge of the chaise, bend the other so that the knee is just a few inches below the fourth grid line of the window frame. The bent leg displays the inner thigh in part of two squares. Her open-toed shoe fills most of one pane.

She looks at the woman reflected in the window, the dark centre of the bare breast visible where the shirt hangs open, the smooth flesh divided by a criss-cross of lines. Any movement will destroy the careful image. The first time she allows Maurice to touch her, it will be here, and she will say, not yet, not yet, and he will not lay a hand on her. She will sit motionless on the chaise, and he will trace her on the window glass, his finger tips moving over the reflected contours of her shoulders, her breasts, her belly, thighs and ankles. The surface will be cool as creek water, and when he finally turns to her, his hands will be the temperature of glass.

Significant Pauses

The nights Gordona works, two men often come in to eat at the Athena, never together, never at the same time. One is tall, dark-haired and thin. His restless fingers fold the placemat into shapes, and the money he leaves on the table is marked by accordion pleats. He speaks to Gordona in her own language, but the conversations are short, and both of them move through the business of ordering and serving food as if their joints have stiffened.

The other is blunt-faced and blond, with the smooth apple cheeks of a boy. His fingers are large-knuckled, his teeth are small and very white, his shoes are always new, he leaves large tips, and he can't keep his eyes off Gordona. I know all this from the times she refuses to serve him and I have to take the table instead. It's been three weeks since I've seen him. Gordona has been away too. She missed several shifts and returned just last week looking strangely pale-skinned around the eyes.

When the blond man returns, I'm on my way to table six, balancing three slippery plates of spaghetti the way Gordona taught me, one resting on my forearm and one in each hand. "Rhea," she says, tossing her head in his direction, "table two." I walk over with the menu and the usual glass of ice water. He takes both with a smile. Tonight, he's wearing a thick cable-knit sweater, and with his hair messed up a little by the wind, he looks as if he stepped right out of a Jacques Cousteau deep-sea diving documentary. I give him a few minutes and then go to take the order. The menu is open in front of him, but he isn't looking at it. He's lighting a cigarette, the same brand Gordona smokes on her breaks, an elegant European cigarette that smells like cow shit set on fire. The couple who were thinking of taking the booth behind him change their minds, veer off and settle several tables away. Gordona is with them in a second, menu ready, ice clinking in the water glasses.

"Can I take your order?"

He exhales more smoke, smiles, waves me away.

I return five minutes later. "If you're ready —"

Again, he waves me away.

Gordona brings the couple a bottle of wine, presents it with a flourish. The woman beckons her closer, whispers in her ear, and Gordona laughs her deep husky laugh. Loud enough that the blond man and I both hear it.

I'm on my way back from the kitchen to ask him a third time when I see him hook two fingers in the air and motion to the manager. I grab a coffee pot and make the rounds, offering a second cup to all the customers. The manager calls Gordona into the small storage room used as an office. She walks out a few minutes later, back rigid, and goes to serve the blond man. When she brings the food, he doesn't eat, just sits there looking at her as she walks among the tables. He motions for coffee. She fills his cup three, four times, takes away his uneaten food, brings him a dessert of sweet baklava resting in a pool of honey. He sits there while Gordona and I close, while I vacuum the bread crumbs from around his feet, then the man and Gordona leave the restaurant at the same time. He uses the front door and she uses the back. The manager waits an extra five minutes for me to wipe the marble top of the bar, then I button my coat and he turns the locks behind the four of us.

I've started to stay at Thomas's place overnight sometimes, crawling into bed beside him when my shift is over. His basement apartment is on the same side of the river as the university, where he is a student. He started out in arts, switched to engineering for a year, then back to arts again, and now he's taking Latin. When he does something he's really sorry for, like the time he forgot to leave the door unlocked and I stood outside for half an hour pounding on the window to wake him, he apologizes in Latin. *Mea culpa.* What he'd really like to study is theology, which is why, he explains, he's interested in celibacy.

"Sex uses too much psychic energy," he says. "I've got to conserve what I have."

So after work tonight, we cuddle for a minute. I tell him about the two men and Gordona, the hungry way they both look at her. We kiss. When the kissing begins to wander, lips moving across territory that's more new to me than it is to him, we stop. He gets up and goes into the kitchen, brews himself a cup of swampy herbal tea and inspects the large multicoloured map of the world that hangs on the wall above the table. Tacks mark the places where the Blessed Virgin has been sighted, colour-coded: red for warnings, green for healing, blue for secrets. Europe bristles with them. Thomas has a story for every tack, and when he tells one of them, he marks our place in the Northern Hemisphere, then slides his finger across the ocean to one of the lucky countries. I listen to him moving around the kitchen and try to get comfortable in the lumpy bed, shifting and turning until my t-shirt is twisted so tight around me that I'm reminded of a picture in one of Mr. Klein's *National Geographic* magazines, a boa constrictor coiled around a helpless goat.

The next day when I get up, I expect him to be gone to classes, but he's home, slumped in the chair with an open newspaper in his lap.

"What is it? Are you sick?"

He points to a small headline: "Farmer Creates Shrine to the Blessed Virgin."

A farmer, recently diagnosed with diabetes, had seen Her

appear above his corn field. Since then, his blood sugars have been steady. I can eat anything I want, he is quoted as saying. Donuts, cinnamon buns, chocolate cake. Anything.

"I'm nearly twenty-eight years old," Thomas keeps repeating, as if there were a biological clock for visions and his has prematurely struck the hour.

The farm with the shrine is in the Eastern Townships of Quebec. "Would it help if you went there?" I ask, thinking of the thick envelope my father tucked into the side pocket of my suitcase the day I left Eyehill. It was full of cash, money he made under the table doing small carpentry jobs for the neighbours. Use it for your education, the note said. There is enough in the envelope to buy a decent car.

The road trip to Quebec is the kind of spontaneous thing that is part of the romance of being with Thomas, and it is romantic, in a way, just the two of us in the small world that is the car. We drive without stopping because we've only got enough money for gas and food. I sleep in short bursts, my head resting on his leg, awakened every now and then by the shift of his muscles when he accelerates.

Neither of us is a good driver. He shoulder checks violently, moves his whole body, moves the steering wheel too, and the car swerves dangerously toward the wrong lane. Mesmerized by the yellow line in the center, I slip into a sort of semi-trance, miss corners, and have to brake abruptly to make the correct turns. Still, we make good time, sliding past small towns and plowed fields. It's late September, the poplar leaves turned golden, the wheat stubble still fresh, the fields along the highway shining yellow in the sun. Back home, my father will be checking the fence on the winter pasture, getting ready to round up the herd and wean the calves. I always gave the vaccinations, prided myself on having a light touch with the needle. I wonder if he'll still hire Jarvis to help with the fall work. He won't see any reason not to, and Jarvis will need the job. My father was bewildered by the way I left, and I didn't explain that Jarvis should have been the one to tell me: By the way, Carmela's two months pregnant. Instead he told my father, and my father told me, and that made me mad at all three of them, especially Carmela: Ever heard of the pill?

The hitchhiker stands on the shoulder just east of Sudbury. I wouldn't consider stopping if I hadn't come so close to hitting the ditch a few miles back. Thomas has been asleep in the back seat for hours, a Gravol-induced coma, and I'm getting a little drowsy myself. I hope the hitchhiker will be a distraction, someone to keep me awake.

The woman is young, maybe my age, maybe a year older, and she's so thin her jeans bunch rather than crease when she settles herself into the seat. She wears a man's muscle shirt, the armholes large and gaping. Sometimes she remembers to clamp her arms tight to her sides, but when she doesn't, the profile of each small breast is clearly visible from the right angle. She's from Winnipeg, going to Toronto, where she has a friend who works in theatre. The friend told her there were more roles in the bigger centres.

"I'd be happy, at first, with small parts," she says. "I know you have to start at the bottom, but what I really want to do are soliloquies with . . ."

Several seconds pass.

Finally she says, "Soliloquies with significant pauses. I want to be the only one on the stage."

We're low on gas and there's an exit coming up. This second lurch of brakes wakes Thomas. He blinks once or twice when he sees another person in the car but says nothing. He's not at his best when newly wakened. I go in to take care of the gas, and when I come out again, Thomas is in the driver's seat, ready for his turn at the wheel. I stop for a second by the passenger door, but the woman doesn't move, so I get in the back seat. Thomas pulls out onto the ramp that curves up toward the highway. The sound of the road blows in the open windows. I stretch out my legs and rest my head on the softness of a rolled up sweatshirt. My eyes are tired of looking for cars that might swerve into wrong lanes or pull out without warning or slam on the brakes unexpectedly.

The woman is talking, coming to the end of a story I missed because I was asleep.

"So I had to be true to myself, you know, as an artist. I told him I wasn't interested in what he had in mind. It wasn't the sex that bothered me, just the size of the audience. I'm not going to waste a performance on just one or two guys. So I left Winnipeg. Started hitching from the Sault because my money for the bus ran out. I've always . . ."

She stops, and I count the silence, the way all of us who took swimming lessons were taught. The instructor gave us each a shot of mouthwash and paired us up. I lay down on my back and Carmela (I won't call her a friend, she was something other than that) knelt down beside me, tilted my head back, and, with the coaching of the instructor, sealed my open mouth with her own, exhaled into my unwilling lungs, then lifted her head while the instructor counted: *one-one thousand, two-one thousand, three-one thousand*, all the way to five, the correct number of seconds between breaths in resuscitation.

". . . always depended on the kindness of strangers."

Thomas nods sympathetically, and before the girl can draw breath to speak again, he begins a story of his own.

"In Yugoslavia, Mary was called Gospa, Queen of Peace. Crowds gathered, hoping to see Her. She appeared only to the six. No one knows why they were chosen." Thomas uses one hand for driving. The other makes gestures to illustrate the story. The hitchhiker and I fix our eyes on the moving hand, like two cats watching the same bird.

"On several occasions, the sun spun on its axis. Each day

the visions appeared a little higher up the mountain. Imagine that, a spinning sun. What would the light have looked like?" Thomas continues, "I read that the same type of thing can happen at the shrine where we're going. People see the sun vibrate."

All the years I lived in Eyehill, I never heard of this vibrating sun.

Thomas's voice again. "Sometimes the people pressed so close, they actually touched the Virgin. But, of course, they couldn't see Her."

An unplowed field, the grass newly mowed, serves as a parking lot for visitors to the shrine. A tour bus is just unloading the last of a group of senior citizens. The hitchhiker is still with us. We offered to let her out at one of the Toronto exits, but she said no, she'd like to go on. I might go as far as Halifax, she says, I have a friend with an apartment there.

The shrine takes up a fair bit of space, most of it a slight hill bordered with a thick stand of flaming red maple trees. First time I've ever seen a real version of the leaf that decorates the flag. The Stations of the Cross are hung with rosaries, garlands of plastic flowers and evidence of healing: pairs of shoes and eyeglasses and the top half of a bikini. Thomas begins to pray his way through the stations with the other pilgrims. A portion of the wooded area on the west side has been thinned and serves as a picnic area. I wander over to wait in the shade.

"Coming?" I ask the hitchhiker, but she shakes her head, watching the others. Before long, she joins them, crossing herself without awkwardness.

I stretch out on my back to watch the leaves. It should be a peaceful place. The murmur of prayer and all that. But it isn't. The air in the clearing is heavy with expectation. The owner of the Athena and several of his friends, guys who owned other restaurants in the city, sometimes gathered late at night to throw dice, and the atmosphere within the circle of trees resembles that of the dice table. Everyone is waiting for something to happen, so I'm not really surprised to hear a bit of commotion over by the fifth station. I join the small crowd that has gathered, easing my way among the seniors to get a better look.

The hitchhiker is swaying slowly, her arms hanging loose by her sides, eyes in a blind stare. She steps right, left, then right again in a sort of pattern, slowly raising her arms until they are above her head, her breasts visible to anyone beside her who knows enough to look into the space created by her over-sized shirt. Thomas is certainly close enough to see them. She turns her face to the sun, points and says, "The clouds are pushed away. Such colours. The sun is . . ."

One-one thousand, two-one thousand, three-one thousand — I time her perfectly, know exactly when she is going to draw breath to continue. *Five-one thousand.*

"The sun is dancing," she gasps, opens her mouth to speak again, then collapses to the ground. Thomas is the first one to reach her. He cradles her head in his lap and calls for water.

An old woman from the tour shares her picnic lunch with me.

"They always pack too much," she says, passing me half a corned beef sandwich. "It was the cancer, spread to his brain, that made him forget everything but the old language. I couldn't understand it, so I called his brother to come to the hospital. We hadn't seen Petar in years, but he came when he heard my husband was dying. What does it mean? I asked. What is he saying? *Mother of God, have mercy*, Petar translated. My husband was petitioning the Blessed Virgin. He never really lost the faith."

Thomas has disappeared from the group. I didn't notice his leaving, but he is definitely gone. Some instinct makes me look over to where the hitchhiker was sitting. She, too, is gone, and somehow I'm not surprised.

"It comforts me to come to places like this," the old woman says, "even if I don't really believe. Even if I never see Her. It's all I have left of him."

Thomas comes out of the woods about half an hour later. He mingles with the elderly pilgrims, his back to me. I can see where his hair curls at the back of his neck, too damp, too much sweat for the temperature of the day. I hear the old woman, but my eyes are fixed on Thomas, watching him make conversation, words about the weather, likely, or other kinds of mysterious powers.

"What brings you here?" she asks.

"Visions. Thomas wants one." I point a finger at his back, singling him out for the old woman. He looks around as though I'd called his name, sees the pointed finger and tries to look unjustly accused.

"Did he have any luck?"

I think of Thomas and the hitchhiker in the red shade of the maples, his hands making their way to those so easily found breasts, her hands on him, here and there, the sounds of their coming together spaced every now and then with significant pauses. *One-one thousand, two-one-thousand,* continuing until that moment when the sun started spinning.

"Did he have one?" she asks again, "Did he have a vision?"

"Sort of. Almost."

"It's nice to know it's not just us old people who are interested in miracles," she says.

A week later, I'm back to work at the Athena, sharing the late shift with an ordinary woman, one with permed hair and a snorting laugh. Several more nights pass before I realize that Gordona is not coming back. I listen to the conversations be-

tween the dishwasher and the cook. I hear the whispers of the
senior waitresses who say, Gordona wore long sleeves in even
the hottest weather, her makeup was too heavy around the
eyes, there are places where women can go, can hide, why does
she stay? Yes, why, why? I joined in, as if all along I'd understood that what was happening was not romance.

Turnbuckle

It is possible that when she was four years old, Sylvie fashioned a boat from a cedar shingle, twigs and a piece of twine. It is possible that she floated it, manned with dandelion flower sailors, on the surface of the duck pond while her little sister crawled on the grass, playing with the ribbons that trailed from a straw hat. Their mother lay nearby, her arm across her eyes to shield them from the sun. There might have been a breeze; something created ripples that lapped around her legs as she waded, tiny movements that tugged at the cedar boat, stretching taut the length of twine that connected it to her hand. Something lifted the straw hat from the ground and set it on the water. The cedar shingle was rectangular, weathered grey on one end, with a nail hole the perfect size for the twig she inserted to act as the mast. It is possible that she navigated the boat through a patch of reeds, as oblivious to the muted thrash of her sister's drowning as she might have been to the faraway bark of a neighbour's dog, while their exhausted mother, diagnosed eventually and too late with an inactive thyroid, slept on.

Sylvie is not a natural blond, but blond is the colour of her hair the first time she meets Winston, at a party in Montreal. He leans against the wall, the only one who isn't dancing, surrounded by bobbing, jerking, twisting people, not one of whom

enters the zone of stillness that surrounds him. He is built like
a wrestler, but her outrageous friend Delphine tells her he's an
architect.

"Oooh," she breathes, "wouldn't you like to get a look at
his flying buttress?"

A few hours later, when the party winds down and Sylvie is
looking for her coat among those piled in a corner, he is the
one who finds it. She is a little drunk, and he holds the coat
open so she can get her arm in the sleeve. She remembers the
conversation going something like this:

"Do you like barns?" he asks.

"Barns?"

"I'm driving to Massachusetts tomorrow to look at a Shaker
barn. Want to come along?"

She looks over his shoulder, across the room to Delphine.
Her friend clasps her hands together, raises them to chest level
and shakes them, first to the right, then to the left, in an
exaggerated gesture of victory.

Sylvie shakes her head no, makes herself dizzy, wobbles on
her heels.

"What about a ride home?"

In the background, her friend becomes unglued, waves her
arms wildly.

"Yes. Yes." Nodding, for Delphine's sake.

He hands her the purse that matches the coat, and they
move toward the door.

"I come from a town smaller than you can imagine," he
says.

She should have known that a funeral, any funeral, is not an
auspicious occasion on which to meet your boyfriend's mother,
but when Winston asked her to make the trip home with him,
all she registered was the crushed look on his face and the
words that came out of his mouth: I need you. She'd felt a

surge of excitement. This was it, what the women's magazines called the Next Step.

Sylvie's first language is French, but she is fluently bilingual, having mastered the harsh rhythm and blended consonants of the English language years ago, as part of a plan she and Delphine had made to find success in New York or Los Angeles. Winston's mother still says the word Canada as if it ends with an r, even though she's lived here for over forty years.

"Welcome to Canada," Queenie says, "such as it is."

They are standing on the steps of St. Jude's, Eyehill's tiny Anglican church. Queenie's hand stretches to show the limits of the short main street: the hotel built in the forties, the Co-op grocery store built in the fifties, the newest building, the Eyehill Café, built just ten years ago. Snow has melted, then frozen, filling the shallow ruts in the unpaved street with ice. The April sunshine is intermittent, but the wind is steady, blowing from the north.

Winston holds the door for his mother and nods to Sylvie to follow. They walk the narrow aisle between the pews toward the altar and the open casket. Even though the dead man's face is slack, the skin an unnatural orange-pink from the under-taker's makeup, Sylvie can see that Winston resembles him. Ernie Bostwick was a stocky man, with a square jaw and dark eyebrows. He is being buried in his uniform.

"He always looked so tidy in it," Queenie says. "That was the army's doing, though I didn't know it then."

Winston reaches out as if he would like to touch his father, but his hand falls short and comes to rest on the shiny oak of the coffin's edge. Sylvie's impulse is to step back, but Winston stands just behind her shoulder, trapping her between himself and his mother. They stand there long enough that the cold from the floor makes itself felt through the thin leather soles of her shoes. The noise of the building fills the silence: the tick of the heater, intermittent soft bangs as the closed door, loose on its hinges, opens and closes a fraction of an inch in the wind.

She is happy to follow Queenie when the older woman turns away and begins walking back up the aisle toward the door. Too late, she realizes that Winston isn't moving from the spot where he stands rigid near his father. She winds up on the concrete step alone with Winston's mother, shivering in her lightweight navy pantsuit, wishing she had brought her winter coat.

"Winston tells me you're an actress," Queenie says.

"Yes."

"In England, before the war, my father used to take us to the theatre."

"I'm in television. Daytime drama."

"He was a typesetter and a very precise man, my father. We took the play books with us and read along to see if the actors remembered their lines."

Sylvie can't think of a thing to say, so she nods.

"It was criminal, really, how many of them couldn't get it right. I'd lost all respect for the profession by the time I was fourteen."

There is a scraping sound as the latch on the door behind them opens. Winston offers one arm to his mother and the other to Sylvie. The three of them descend the slippery steps together.

At the lunch that follows the interment, Sylvie is offered egg salad sandwiches and butter tarts. She stands off to the side as person after person comes to offer condolences to Winston and Queenie. A man about the same age as Winston shakes hands with him, then draws him close in a rough, one-armed sort of hug. Sylvie admires Queenie's posture. Back pats, hand shakes, the occasional embrace, not one of these dislodges the imaginary book that balances on the older woman's head. The women who pass the sandwiches try not to stare at Sylvie's pantsuit and her fluffy blond hair, but she can see them whispering among themselves as they refill the empty plates with date squares and cherry balls.

Is that her?

You know, the actress Winston's dating. The one in the French soap opera. They say she plays the good daughter.

The place where Winston lived his first twelve years is now abandoned, littered with old machines, all of them rusty, many of them unidentifiable.

"What are those things that look like giraffes?" Sylvie asks.

"Augers. They move the grain upward into the bin with this corkscrew mechanism."

Winston points to the spiral within the long, neck-like tube. She can see, even though the metal is weathered, that the edges of the spiral are sharp.

"A boy I went to school with lost his arm in one of these," he says.

The top of the auger, the part that looks like the head of the giraffe, is fitted with a hinged lower jaw. The metal flaps in the wind that blows through the piston guts of the decaying tractors. Chains bang against metal. The loose arm of a combine spout creaks back and forth.

"My father was forever buying junk. Just needs a little adjustment, he'd say, tighten a belt, clean the spark plugs. Good as new." Winston jerks his head toward the chaos of the yard. "He always planned to double his money."

The house is gone, moved off its foundation and sold for use as a granary on another, more prosperous farm. Last summer's dead grass pokes through piles of boards and shingles that once were outbuildings, one end of a peaked roof all that is recognizable. The barn still stands, red paint clinging here and there to the wide grey boards. Winston leads her to the big sliding door that hangs on a track. One of the bottom corners is flush with the cracked concrete pad beneath it, while the other shows a four-inch gap.

"That space," he says, "is there because all barns, especially old barns, have a life of their own. The door stays square on the track, but the barn leans one way or another, depending on the wind. Another time, that gap might not be there, or it might be the other corner that has lifted."

Winston leans his weight against the edge of the door, and it rolls a foot or two along the track before it jams. The space is wide enough that they can slip through the opening.

"We never had cows, and the horses were gone before my time. But my mother kept chickens."

The sound of the wind becomes the sound of wood, the creak of joists and rafters. A sparrow flies past her shoulder, rests briefly on the sill of a broken window, then is sucked into the sky. Winston reaches into a manger and brings out a large wrench, then leads her to a ladder. She climbs and he follows.

Up in the loft, the sound of wood moving against wood is magnified by the emptiness, and their voices echo in the space. She wonders if she is imagining a slight rocking movement beneath her feet. She looks up, checking the roof, expecting the small chinks and cracks of light to widen before her eyes. Beside her, Winston's head is bent toward the floor. She sees what he sees, a series of steel cables running across the floorboards, connecting the left wall to the right in four places. A turnbuckle sits at the centre of each cable.

"Barns collapse beneath the weight of their roofs," he says. "My buddy Quinn and I worked one whole summer on this barn. Every few weeks, we'd come up here and wind the cables a little tighter."

A gust comes in the open west window. Winston kneels beside the turnbuckle, fits the wrench over the screw mechanism, then puts the force of his body's weight into pulling on the wrench. His voice comes in fits and starts, a reflection of the effort required.

"Works. Best. On windy days."

Sylvie feels her body tighten. She is caught, made speechless by the perfect flex, his arms.

"We pulled the east wall eight inches."

Winston rests back on his heels for a minute, not looking at her, his eyes still focused on the turnbuckle, the way his hands grasp the wrench.

"My mother hated the chickens, called them filthy birds, but we needed the egg money. The job at the post office was her deliverance."

Sylvie watches as he winds the turnbuckle tighter with another quarter turn of the wrench, neck and shoulder muscles bulging with the strain.

"She saved every penny to send me away."

Sylvie and Winston and Delphine walk a winding garden path that leads to a miniature house made of brown and green and clear glass bottles. They have been invited for drinks with a friend of Winston's, another architect. Winston's idea. He thought, perhaps Delphine and Douglas?

"Are you familiar with St. Maclou?" Douglas asks.

"I'm an atheist," Delphine says.

"It's a building." Winston is pouring wine.

"A Gothic cathedral that would never have been possible if the pointed arch had not become an integral part of the ribbed groin vault." Douglas takes a sip of wine. "Amazing. They could cover any shape. Pentagon. Trapezoid. Imagine a church made of lace. Imagine a building that is as much about the openings in the stone as the stone itself."

"Lingerie," Winston says, "that church always made me think of lingerie."

Douglas pours himself another glass of wine. "It was the stained glass of the clerestory and my own passion for recycling that inspired all this. I started it as a playhouse for my son." He looks at the empty bottle. "Excuse me," he says, "There's another one over at the house."

"His wife left him three years ago," Winston says.

"He has a child? That does it," Delphine says. "I decided a long time ago I wasn't having children."

Winston shoots a look at Sylvie.

She recognizes it as a question. Her free hand, the one not holding the drink, moves just enough that Winston can see the nearly imperceptible rise of her index and middle fingers. knowing even as she does it that the gesture is a lie.

Two children.

The thought of giving birth reminds her of one of the first roles she tried out for, a small part in a science fiction series. She had to stand perfectly still while a Plexiglas cylinder descended from the ceiling and encased her. She couldn't do it. Too bad, one of the stage hands said as she was dismissed from the set, there's at least five minutes worth of air in there. You wouldn't suffocate.

Douglas is back, whistling, stooping to enter through the small door.

Delphine holds her glass out for a refill, examines her arm mottled green in the murky light and says, "Anyone else feel as if you're underwater?"

Sylvie's second visit to Eyehill is in winter, the week before Christmas. She'd wanted to go skiing in the Laurentians, but Winston wasn't interested. He has been gone all afternoon, helping Quinn and some others repair the roof of the skating rink. She and his mother stand shoulder to shoulder in Queenie's small kitchen, sharing a sink. She is peeling potatoes and the older woman is washing lettuce for a salad. The window above the sink gives a view of the empty alley that runs behind the Co-op store, the Eyehill Hotel, and the other buildings on the west side of Main Street. On the windowsill, there is a pot of African violets and a small framed picture of a man leaning against a lamp post, grinning for the camera. The background is full of buildings and shop signs. Queenie sees her looking at the photograph.

"Ernie," she says, "taken in London, before we were married." She shakes water from the lettuce before setting it on a cutting board, then takes a butcher's knife and begins to cut. Lettuce falls away from the blade in thin shreds. "I keep it for the signs as much as anything." She points the tip of the knife at some blurred letters in the background. "Sillitoe's Fine Hats and Accessories. I worked there as a milliner's assistant, attaching the veils and feathers, doing a bit of beading. We once did up a hat for the Queen Mother, the Duchess of York she was then."

"I wish hats were still in style," Sylvie says.

"They don't suit everyone," her mother-in-law says, glancing at Sylvie, evaluating the shape of her face and the size of her ears.

"There were days when all I did was attach black veils to black hats. The War . . ."

Queenie trails off, concentrating on the lettuce. The light coming in the window is dimming, a combination of increasing cloud and setting sun. A truck parks in the alley and three men get out. Winston is one of them. They walk away from the house, toward the bar in the Eyehill Hotel.

"The War changed how we dressed, what we ate, how we slept. My mother moved all the beds away from the windows, crowded them all into the center of the house after she heard about a man whose throat was cut by flying glass when bombs fell nearby."

Twilight has drained all the colour from the street. Grey roofs, white snow, black tree trunks. The view through the window matches the old photograph. Ernie Bostwick. Black hair, white teeth, the grey bricks of London all around him.

"Before he asked me to marry him, Ernie took me for a walk around the East End. Parts of it were nothing but rubble. We walked on and on, him looking down most of the time, counting steps. I'd worn my sister's shoes, a size too small, and my feet were starting to blister by the time we stopped. That's how much land I own in Canada, he said. That's the size of my farm."

Sylvie watches as the clerk from the Co-op comes out the back door, bends and plugs in an extension cord. A string of red Christmas lights comes on.

"I thought of all the people that much of the East End used to hold, all the houses and flats and churches and shops. When he lived through his last posting, I thought, There now, I'll marry him and be set for life."

She flips a switch, turning on the light over the sink so she can better see to shred the last of the lettuce from the core. Eyehill disappears into darkness, becomes a backdrop, a frame within the window frame for the picture of Ernie Bostwick and his I've-got-the-world-by-the-tail grin.

In semi-darkness, Sylvie leans against a set of papier-mâché boulders, the walls of an underground passage. Earlier, the makeup girl applied brown smears to her cheeks. A man paces back and forth in front of her. She used to rest her top teeth on her bottom lip during lulls in conversation. The camera made this habit look ridiculous, and it was the first thing she had to change when she landed the part of DeeDee on *Secret de famille*. DeeDee has a wicked mother and a nasty sister. In the eight years she's been on the show, she has lost four boyfriends, three to her sister and one to her mother. Her nasty sister, Aurora, has been in two car accidents, has been lost in a mountain cave, has pretended to be pregnant, has threatened to end the false pregnancy with a false abortion, has pretended to be paralyzed and has slept with nine men, including a father and his son, the son being engaged to DeeDee at the time.

When she walked in on her sister in bed with her fiancé, the director gave this advice: Look shocked.

Today, DeeDee is bound and gagged, once again a victim, not of her mother and sister for a change, but of a man who seems to be a total stranger. Of course, he will turn out to be someone that somebody knows. The writers are very close-mouthed about their plots, but rumour has it that the man may be DeeDee's biological father.

The gag is making Sylvie feel nauseous.

The man stops pacing.

For over a week now, the smell of coffee from the cast lounge has made her stomach heave. Hurry up, she thinks. Get on with it. She goes over her line in her head, trying to ward off the unexpected sickness. Unexpected. Expected. Expecting.

He kneels in front of her and holds her face in his hands for a moment, before moving them behind her head to undo the gag.

"Who are you?"

"Don't you know me, DeeDee?"

She shakes her head. Expecting. Could she be?

"It's me, your father. Your real father."

"Look shocked," the director says.

Delphine surprises Sylvie with the information that she had an abortion a few years back.

"I didn't tell you because I knew you would think of it as a death," she says, "and you are a little funny about death."

The little white stick (called the wand by the home pregnancy test, as if it were magic) sits on the glass top of Delphine's coffee table. She'd asked Delphine to read the instructions from outside the closed bathroom door, while she, inside, looked at the line that showed itself, stark and blue in the little white window.

"I'll go with you to the clinic," Delphine says.

"It seems unfair not to tell Winston."

"Do what you want," Delphine says, "but if you tell him, be prepared."

"For what?"

"Men are surprisingly old-fashioned."

Sylvie looks again at the pregnancy test. "I was so careful. I never missed a pill."

"It's just a blue line," Delphine says. "Think of it that way and you'll feel better."

Sylvie meets Winston at his apartment later that night.

"You look pale," he says. "Can I get you something?"

She hasn't eaten much all day. There is no enlargement of her body, no outward sign of the pregnancy, but the secret fills her so full she has trouble swallowing.

"I'll make you a grilled cheese sandwich," he says.

She watches him as he moves around the small kitchen, sees him from the back, his body compact, wide shoulders, neat ass, his legs well muscled beneath the pants. He slices cheese from a block.

"Did I ever tell you about the first time I worked on a barn? I was twelve."

"That seems young."

"We wanted to. There was Quinn and me and four men. The men had harnesses, but they built a makeshift rig for Quinn and me, tied us together with a length of rope. Then they put us one on each side of the peak, Quinn on the east and me on the west, the rope across the space between us. Quinn's father taught me how to lay shingles with the right amount of overlap, and how to nail blocks of two-by-four to create footholds that you could move as you moved up the roof."

Sylvie watches his hand, the way his fingers radiate from his palm in a half circle as he uses the span between his thumb and little finger to roughly measure the width of an imaginary board. He drops a gob of butter in the hot pan.

"I got cocky. Wanted to work faster than Quinn, wanted to impress the men, and I pounded just one nail into the center of the blocks I was using for footholds instead of two like I'd been told. If I was careful with my feet, one was enough." He pauses to transfer a sandwich from the counter to the pan. "The roof was shingled almost to the peak when I slipped. Skidded down the slope, shirt bunched up around my neck. Couldn't see. Couldn't grab hold of anything because there was nothing to hold."

Sylvie wants to say she knows exactly how that feels. He flips the sandwich in the pan. "I jerked to a stop, my shins banging against the eaves. I looked up to see Quinn braced against the cupola. His weight was all that saved me."

Sylvie thinks of the horizontal blue line of the pregnancy test, then of the umbilical cord, the thread of flesh that anchors the baby within her, and she comes back to the rope that saved Winston, delivered him to her eighteen years later.

"My father wasn't on the roof at the time. He was fiddling with the truck radio, trying to get better reception. I dangled from the roof, and there was a sudden blare of music, a woman's twang. My father said, Patsy Cline. Listen up boys, that'll make your dinks fly out."

Sylvie looks down to where her hand presses into the soft spot beneath the meeting of her ribs. The actress in her wonders if it would be too melodramatic to take Winston's hand and place it there, over her own.

"He didn't even see me," Winston says, setting out a plate.

"Come here," she says. "I have something to tell you."

"Large weddings are a lot of showy nonsense, especially under the circumstances." Queenie takes a handful of peanuts from a cut glass dish and eyes Sylvie's belly, still flat four months into the pregnancy. "Let me have a look at that list."

They are sitting on hard-backed chairs around the dining room table. In less than two weeks, Queenie will have a series of strokes, the last of which will rob her of the ability to connect a name to a face, one of many small losses. The peanuts will be blamed, as well as the salt the old woman sprinkles generously on everything she eats, including buttered bread. The wedding date will be postponed to allow for her recovery, but in the end, they will get married without her.

She scans the list, grinding the peanuts with her back teeth. She nods.

Sylvie is relieved. There are nine people on the list: Winston, Sylvie, Quinn, his wife Maggie, Delphine and her poet, Sylvie's landlady and her daughter to act as flower girl, and, of course, Queenie.

"Who is Delphine? Your sister?"

"A friend. Is there anyone you'd like to add?"

"By rights, I should invite Phyllis and her husband, and the woman who fills in for me when I'm sick, but she'd need her son to fly to Montreal with her, because of her arthritis, and that would make thirteen." She pauses for a moment. "Will there be a meal?"

"Yes, of course. Right at the hotel."

"Too unlucky."

"We're not superstitious."

"Not worth it. It's my son's first marriage. Phyllis will understand, and she'll organize the quilt, all the same."

"The quilt?"

"The ladies always make a quilt. And there will be a collection for you at the Co-op. Phyllis will type the names of everyone who contributes on a piece of wide white ribbon. I

still have mine. A little keepsake. I'm sure Winston will ap-
preciate it."

She looks at the list again, checking it as she would a stamp
for a postmark, then looks at Sylvie.

"My father moved back to the States before I went to
school. My mother is dead."

"So you're like Winston. An only child."

"Yes."

Early in their relationship, she had gone through all this with
Winston. She told him she cannot remember much about her
sister or her sister's death by drowning. She was too young.
The only thing I know for sure, she told him, is that there was
a pond and that the dandelion flowers were plentiful and very
yellow.

Sylvie didn't want to come to this party in the Eyehill Community Hall, arranged just before the baby was born.

"I'll go alone," Winston said.

"Why can't they wait six months?"

"You know what the doctor said when he called. He said her
brain was a time bomb. He could practically hear it ticking."

So now she is in a large cold room, its doorways draped
with streamers and tissue bells for Queenie's birthday. The old
woman sits at a special table, on a cushion to soften her chair.
She had her hair done yesterday and slept in a plastic cap to
preserve the curl. Sylvie sits as far back from the activity as her
place to the left of her mother-in-law at the head table allows,
shifting her weight from side to side to ease the ache she still
feels in her perineum, hoping the movement will soothe the
baby. Zoë sleeps in short stretches, two hours, one hour, twenty
minutes. Sylvie feels the interrupted nights as a slight vibration throughout her body, a background hum of tiredness. She
hopes she doesn't look as wild-eyed as she feels. The night

before their flight, during the brief hours that Zoë slept, Sylvie lay awake, imagining the plane spiralling downward, Winston unconscious, herself with two broken legs, the baby helpless and unrescued.

Quinn is speaking to Queenie. Something about letters to Santa Claus.

"Everyone knows it was you who wrote those letters," he says. "You always ended them the same way. Be a good boy and remember your duty to family and country."

Queenie gives him the same smile she has given all the others.

The baby fusses intermittently. Sylvie shifts her from the crook of her right arm to the crook of her left and adjusts the flannel blanket. Winston has gone to the back room to get a few more chairs because the crowd is larger than expected.

An older woman approaches with a camera.

"We must have a picture of this," she says. "Three generations."

When the flash goes off, Zoë startles as if she's been shot. Eyes open, mouth open, spine stiff, she begins to scream. Heads turn to look at them. Sylvie leans over on her chair, afraid to take her eyes off the baby, her free hand scrabbling to find the diaper bag. When her fingers finally make contact with the bag, she bends her head to look at it, to locate the zipper, and in that moment of inattention, another woman, the one who has been collecting dirty teacups, moves in and scoops Zoë away.

"There, there, sweetheart. There."

She holds the baby in one arm and somehow tightens the wrap of the receiving blanket with her free hand. Sylvie half rises, unsure of how to get Zoë back, as the woman brings Zoë's head to rest against her shoulder and presses her cheek to the baby's head, all of it one-armed. She begins a song without words, an improvised la-la-la, her second arm outstretched, the hand moving back and forth in a gentle movement, as if she were conducting an orchestra that accompanies her singing. Her feet move, right, left, right, and her knees bend slightly to the rhythm of a waltz.

Sylvie is paralyzed.

The woman begins to spin. Zoë stops crying.

Winston walks toward the table, carrying a stack of six chairs. Sylvie tries to call out to him, her mouth opens, freezes at the beginning of a word.

"La-la, la-la-la-la."

Winston sets down the chairs and approaches the woman. He taps her on the shoulder.

"May I cut in?"

She hands the baby over with a smile, still singing. Winston box steps his way toward Sylvie.

Babies can die. When she watched the obstetrician take the child from between her legs, her first thought was of the duck pond, because of the way the baby flailed against the air of the delivery room, still fighting her way through water and murk toward life. She sags a bit when Winston places Zoë in her arms, but she straightens. She looks at the circle of women and nods politely to each in turn. She can make herself cry, she can make herself not.

The two women sit opposite each other, exhausted by the party, Queenie on the couch and Sylvie in the platform rocker, nursing Zoë. Winston placed a tea tray on the low table in front of the couch, set with tiny silver tongs to pluck the cubes of sugar from the bowl and tiny silver spoons for stirring. He arranged lemon wedges on a china plate, then disappeared into the kitchen and slipped out of the house. Sylvie heard the porch door closing.

She is trying to keep the receiving blanket pinned between her shoulder and the back of the chair. The baby does not like even the soft confinement of the blanket's flannel tent, she waves an arm and wiggles, breaking the latch she had on the breast. Sylvie pulls her to the breast again, rocking gently in the chair. The baby settles. The thermostat is set at eighty degrees, and the heat in the room increases the low-level lightheadedness she has lived with since Zoë was born. She thinks of washing a wool sweater by hand. Why wool? The heaviness of it, the effort required to lift it from a tub of water.

Queenie examines the silver tongs, turning them over in her hands. The tea that Winston poured sits cooling in her cup.

The chair emits a low, rhythmic grinding noise as it slides back and forth on its rockers. Warmth spreads along the soles of her feet, her toes still chilled by the draft that swept across the hall floor every time a new guest arrived.

"Such a nice party," Sylvie says. "I thought the macaroons were especially lovely." The cookies had, in fact, been slightly burned at the edges. She mentions them hoping for the usual cutting retort from Queenie, for words with an edge to keep her awake.

Queenie turns the tongs over in her hands.

"How will that child be fed and clothed?" she asks.

Sylvie stops rocking for a moment, trying to clear her head, to understand the question.

"Pardon?"

The old woman brings the tongs close to her face, examining the inner surfaces. "Whatever this is, it might be worth something," she says. "Do you think we could sell it?"

Tick. Tick. The wall clock. If only Zoë would cry. But the baby nurses, drowsy and content.

"What concerns me most is the food," her mother-in-law says. "We can make do with everything else. What to use for food. Formula is so expensive."

"Winston makes a good living."

"Winston?"

"Yes."

"Winston." The sound of her son's name seems to calm Queenie. "At least there are no bombs," she says. "Nothing

worth bombing on this God-forsaken farm. He might go
hungry, but he'll never wake up crying at the sound of a bomb."

"Winston?"

"Yes."

The old woman sets the tongs aside and tucks herself up
on the couch, pulling a crocheted afghan over herself.

Zoë stirs a little and Sylvie resumes her rocking. Her feet,
even the ends of her toes, pulse with warmth. She feels sweet
relief as the baby drains the breast, which had grown painfully
engorged at the party. Her head drops forward, jerks up again.
Since Zoë's birth, before even, in the last months of her
pregnancy, she has kept vigil, convinced that wakefulness is the
glue, the only thing that keeps her world from coming apart.
She must not sleep. She might drop the baby.

She must not sleep, but the clock, the rocker, the noise each
makes becomes distant. She doesn't see him, doesn't hear him
until he is right beside her. She lifts her eyelids a fraction of an
inch, enough to watch as his hands pull aside the blanket and
reach for Zoë. She smells something that isn't quite horses or
hay or leather or sap, a dusty smell that is more memory of
animals than animal itself. The weight of the baby eases from
her lap.

"Shh," he says.

Winston. Bent over the turnbuckle, winding, winding, pulling the walls of the old barn inward, holding them together
with the strength of his back.

Zigzag Fence

Tony clamps the seed between his teeth, testing it the way his grandfather used to test a kernel of wheat for moisture, feeling it yield slightly to the pressure of his bite. Feels good, has a meaty texture and leaves no trace of mould on his tongue. The others in the bag look the same. A good batch.

Sweet jesus, he loves spring.

Loves it in a liquid way, all sap and surge and swell, like an animal must, like a deer nosing the soil for that first taste of green.

Tony learned all he knows about growing from two men: his grandfather and Ganja Man. His grandfather used to say he knew this pasture better than he knew his own wife. One box stall of the old man's barn was filled with deer antlers he collected as he criss-crossed the land, checking the fences for broken wire and the cow herds for foot rot and bloat. If he were still alive, it would be impossible to hide the plots from him.

Ganja was an old hippie, a back-to-the-lander who bought the McDermott place and lived in Eyehill for five years, from the time Tony was fifteen until he turned twenty. Ganja wanted two things: to be self-sufficient and to write a book about growing. Not just any book, he'd say. A philosophical book, a long ode to the kind weed.

The cows sold years ago, after his grandfather died, and now the ungrazed pasture runs to brush: wolf willow, buffalo berry, chokecherry, wild roses. Tony kneels at the edge of a four-by-four-foot square of brown earth, hidden from view on three sides by the scrubby bushes. Plots like this one are scattered throughout the three hundred acres. He sifts the soil through his fingers, taking the temperature of the sun-warmed dirt, smoothing it, using the end of a pencil to press shallow holes in the soil.

The buds on the plants grown from the seeds Ganja left behind will be potent, not as strong as what sells on the street, but strong enough. Tony has a friend in Edmonton bring him a bag every now and then, and he smokes it for the sake of comparison, the way a rancher might occasionally order a chicken burger to see how it stacks up against the beef. Last few years, the street stuff seems too strong, takes him beyond a nice warm high into some other, colder place. And most of it is grown hydroponically. Plenty of chemical and no soil at all. Tony is too much a student of Ganja Man to be all right with that.

He pushes a seed, pointed end upward, into each of the holes. The sun shines on his back, warming his skin through the flannel of his shirt, warming the silver leaves of the wolf willow, releasing the scent of its tiny blossoms.

Spring. He loves it with his lungs, his liver, the soles of his feet. He loves it like he loved Roxanna when he was seventeen.

Joseph Lafonde's wife whispers from habit, even though the kids are away, spending the night with their aunt.

"We should have sex."

"Tonight?"

"When else? It will be the last time."

Roxanna lifts her t-shirt over her head with both arms, showing off her red lace bra and the breasts that fill it. Red is her favourite colour. It used to have two curved wires hidden under the lace, one beneath each breast, but a few months ago, he took the sharp end of his jackknife, made tiny slits in the seams and took the wires out. He did this with all the bras he found in her dresser drawer.

"I'd like to enjoy it," she says.

He unbuttons his shirt.

"But I feel a little sick. Nervous about tomorrow."

"Should you take something?"

She nods, pushes her jeans down past her knees, steps out of them and starts walking to the bathroom. He removes his own jeans, watching the sway of her hips before she disappears through the door. He looks down at the faded grey cotton of his undershorts, his flesh slack beneath the cloth.

When she comes back, he is in bed, covers pulled to his waist.

"Want me to get the light?"

"Okay."

She flips the switch and stretches out beside him.

"Tell me. What was your favourite time?"

He's embarrassed. "Too many."

"Pick one."

"That night at the fairgrounds. On the floor of the horse trailer."

She gives a quick, quiet laugh, belly rising once, twice. "You're so romantic."

"I spread clean straw. I laid a blanket." He thinks of the black space made by the metal walls of the trailer, the way the laughter and screams of the people riding the midway floated through the small high windows, the sound of the horses cropping grass just outside. Her skin, the smell of cotton candy on her fingers.

"That was a good time," she says.

"What about you?"

She rubs her thumb across his knuckles. Finally, she says, "On the slope of the gully. In the snow." The Valium is kicking in, making her words come slowly, with careful hesitations between each one.

"Come on," he says, "I didn't really ask you to do it in the snow." He remembers warm grass on the sunny side of the gully, small icy patches still melting in the shadows of the low spots.

"I had one hand in snow the whole time."

He feels her body shift, as if beginning to turn toward him. He's ready, thanks to the memory of the horse trailer, bulging in the confines of his shorts. He lifts himself on his elbow. She's still on her back, eyes closed. He lays a hand lightly on her shoulder. Slowly, slowly, she turns her head until the skin of her cheek touches his fingers. He stays in that position, hunkered over her as she sleeps, until the pins and needles in the arm that supports his weight force him to shift. Light from a thin moon shines into the room, enough that he can see the rise and fall of her chest beneath the sheet. He sits up and reaches over to the bed table, then settles his back against the headboard, the alarm clock resting in his hand.

Nine o'clock tomorrow morning. The mastectomy. Don't be late.

Tony's first visit to Ganja's derelict farm house has nothing to do with pot. Word in Eyehill is that Ganja used to play guitar with a rock band in BC. Tony knocks on the door, hoping the stranger will give him lessons. He wants to learn a particular song.

A woman answers. She's got long hair twisted into two braids. She's holding something that looks like a small club. Tony steps back.

"Oh, this," she says. "Just a pestle. I'm pounding up some nut butter."

"Don't look so scared, kid," Ganja says, coming up behind her. "She's not talking about your nuts. Mine maybe. Not yours." He looks at the guitar in Tony's hand.

"Come on in."

The woman leaves for another part of the house. Ganja takes

Tony into the living room. There is no couch, just a mattress on the floor. A television sits in the corner, snakes of antenna wire coiled to one side of it. Tony chooses to sit on an overturned five-gallon pail. Ganja drops onto the mattress. For a second, a whiff of something that smells like a prairie fire fills the air.

"Come to the wrong place for a little jammin'. I left my guitar in White Rock."

"I heard you played."

"So I did. So I did. What did you have in mind?"

"Sweeney Todd."

"I used to drink beer with Nick himself."

"I want to learn to play 'Roxy Roller.'"

Ganja leans back against the wall. He narrows his eyes at Tony, looks at him for a long time.

"A girl, right?"

Tony stares back at him.

"You want to impress a girl. I've seen it all before, kid, some of it in my own mirror. Don't look so guilty. Love's a wonderful thing."

He has no idea what to say. The word love sounds strange, coming from the lips of a man who must be over forty, as old as Tony's father. Ganja's gaze slides around the room, past Tony, toward the blank TV screen.

"What's her name?"

"Roxanna."

Tony's neck is starting to heat up under the collar of his jean jacket. Part of him wants to get away. Another part wonders if this strange man might reveal things that could help him, things to do with sex. The woman who answered the door had a hickey on her neck.

"What?" Ganja asks, as if he hadn't heard.

"Roxanna."

"Feels good to say it again, don't it?"

The sound of rhythmic pounding, coming from the woman in the kitchen.

Ganja's gaze makes a slow, jerky journey back toward the five gallon pail.

"Yeah. Love. Nothing to do with music."

Joseph eases his truck from the University Hospital parking lot, turns right and joins the traffic heading over the bridge toward the setting sun and a handful of high-rises, indigo silhouettes that make up the downtown. The car ahead of him hesitates as it exits the bridge, and Joseph leans on the horn.

He passes through the centre of the city, looking for one of the bars he used to visit when he was underage. There it is. Different name, but the building still serves the same purpose; the neon sign blinks Thirsty's, and a neon horse gallops beneath the letters, legs flashing a cold blue. Another sign, hand-lettered, is positioned at the entrance to the parking lot. Outriders Welcome. He wheels his truck in beside it.

When he was a younger man, Joseph got into bar fights. Over nothing. Some guy would walk a little too close, bump him with a shoulder or an elbow, the impact not even enough to spill the drink he held in his hand, but his temper would arc like a welding rod. He was often outweighed in these scuffles, but he threw a fast punch and never lost his footing.

He lets the motor idle, his hands loose on the wheel.

Best to treat this type of cancer aggressively, the doctors say. That's why they cut so much away. That's why she's in hospital for the first few days of chemotherapy. To see how much she'll tolerate.

Go home, she said.

He feels guilty because yesterday, when she was turning herself inside out and there was nothing he could do to stop it, he wanted to go, and he thinks she read him like a book.

Go. Look after the kids. It's what I want you to do.

What he wants to do right now is walk into the bar, catch the eye of a man he doesn't know and stare the stranger down.

After a while, the guy will stop on his way to get another drink and say, What are you looking at? He will say, Nothing. Answer me, asshole, the other guy will say, I said, what are you looking at?

He wants to pick someone sitting with lots of buddies ready to jump in if it looks like Joseph is going to win the fight. He knows he could knock down the first guy. Maybe the second one, too. But in the end, what he really wants is to lose, to come away from the bar and go back to the hospital with a cracked rib or a broken jaw. They could take X-rays, give him pictures of his own bones made real as hockey cards. He could hold the fractures in his hand and offer them up, like something to trade.

Tony can't remember if he ever told Laney about Roxanna. He and Laney have been together, what? Seven years? Ever since she moved from Saskatoon and started her job as a nurse at the Airedale Hospital. Eight years, maybe, since she threaded the needle the doctor used to sew up the gash left on his shin when he misjudged the distance between a plant and his leg and cut himself with the sickle. A sickle, she said, who uses a sickle in this day and age?

Midday sun leaks into the kitchen around the edges of the window blinds, lays a few narrow stripes of light across the countertop where Tony's making sandwiches. She's sitting at the kitchen table, sorting the mail she just picked up in town. It's her salary that will pay most of the bills, because Tony doesn't like to deal anymore, not the way he used to when he worked with Ganja, when most of the people buying were older than him.

"They say Roxanna Lafonde is pretty sick."

Tony freezes in the act of plugging in the kettle.

"No coffee for me. Getting to be too hot outside. Anyway, I had one in town this morning."

He must have told her. He tells her just about everything.

"I'm looking in my purse for change to pay for the coffee when Phyllis asks me what I think Roxanna's chances are. I'm just a nurse, I say, not an oncologist. You know what people are like. A few weeks ago it was old Mrs. Schektel's daughter asking me, Was it true that her son could catch chicken pox from his grandmother if the old lady had shingles? I'm not an epidemiologist."

He places a ham slice on a piece of bread. Laney collects antique tin containers, and they keep their pot and rolling papers in a tea canister celebrating the Coronation. Tony was drunk when Ganja rolled him his first joint, drunk and flat on his back, lying on the ragged patch of grass behind Ganja's house, tears rolling down his cheeks, crying like a goddamn girl. He remembers the older man showing him how to inhale, how to hold the smoke in his lungs for the time it took to sing "Happy Birthday" in his head. The kind weed smoothes, Ganja said. The kind weed smoothes us all.

He cuts the sandwich into triangles and puts the dirty knife into the sink. Laney is opening envelopes. He unfolds a cigarette paper, takes a pinch of marijuana out of the tin, rolls, twists. Three plates set out on the counter top: one for his sandwich, one for Laney's and one for the two perfect joints he just rolled.

She clears the mess from the table.

"What do you think?" he asks.

She lifts the bread off the top of her sandwich. "Too much mayo."

"I mean about Roxanna."

She reaches for the mustard. "If she's got as much cancer as they say, her chances can't be good." She nudges the plate with the joints in his direction. "You want yours before or after?"

"Desire mutates," Ganja said. The woman who met Tony the first time he knocked on Ganja's door is gone, packed up and left just before spring thaw.

"So, kid, now I need a hand with the growing. Interested?"

The older man works the plot of chest-high plants, his body bared to the waist, a strip of bandanna tied around his forehead. Skinny arms, skinny legs, the tendons clearly visible, the mechanics of his body revealed in the bend of a knee or elbow. He has a slow, deliberate way of moving that makes him good at demonstrations. Tony's skin itches in places where the sweat collects, his running shoes feel too tight, he hasn't had anything to drink since morning, and his head is starting to buzz.

He shows Tony how to sex the plants. They work their way through the leaves, bending the plants this way and that.

"Male." Ganja says, showing Tony the tiny cluster of pollen balls.

It's Tony's job to cut the male plants off at the root. He uses the sickle he found hanging from a nail in his grandfather's barn. In each plot, Ganja leaves one male to pollinate the females and provide the seed for next year's crop.

"See that?" he says, pointing to an insignificant cluster, the white stigmas slender as threads. "Female. Three or four weeks and that will be a bud."

Tony tosses the male plant aside.

"Life imitates pot," Ganja says, pointing to the growing pile of cut plants. "Those are smokable, but it's the female who intoxicates, who wields the heady power in her buds."

The buzz in Tony's head grows louder. Nearly a year now since Roxanna cut him loose.

"Smoke break?" he asks.

Ganja nods, his eyes still on the plant in front of him.

"Remember this. The weed wants a loving touch." Ganja holds the pointed end of a leaf gently between his thumb and forefinger. "Just like a woman."

When the kids were little and throwing tantrums, Roxanna stood at the sink, peeling potatoes, impervious to the screaming, the drumming heels, the head-banging. The kids are like him. Firecrackers. Eventually, they exhausted themselves and grew quiet.

See, she'd said to Joseph, there's no need to spank them.

This morning, once the kids are away to school, she insists on going to town with him. The fruit trucks from BC are making a last pass through Eyehill, stopping for a few hours on their way to Airedale and other larger towns. She takes one of his old wild rags, the red silk he used to knot around his neck when he raced horses, and winds it around her head.

"What do you know about fruit?" she asks. "The pears you bought at the grocery store were already rotten in the center."

He gives her a boost up into the passenger side of the four-wheel drive. The surface of the road is marked by small bumps and hollows, the last traces of ruts baked hard by hot sun and dry weather. She rolls down the window a crack and takes deep breaths of air.

Coming down the small hill that slopes onto Main Street, he slows, sees the fruit truck parked near the Co-op store. A grey-haired woman is setting out the last of the season's peaches and pears, twenty-pound boxes. She waves, but Roxanna isn't looking. She's using the rear view mirror to adjust the scarf.

He reaches across his wife's thin torso to flick open the passenger door. She gets out carefully, slowly, one foot on the ground and then the other.

"At least let me get the groceries," he says. "I've got a list, for christ's sake."

She nods.

"Roxanna," the fruit lady calls, waving. The same truck's been coming for years.

A gust of wind plasters his wife's t-shirt to her chest, emphasizing, for a moment, the unnatural size of her breasts. The prosthesis was made to fit the body she had before the chemo started to pare the flesh from her. No point in building another, the technician said. Once the treatments are over, she'll put the weight back on.

He takes his list into the store. Phyllis, the only clerk, lifts her chin toward the large window that gives a clear view of the street.

"Good to see her out."

He's working his way back toward the front of the store, stopped by the shelf that holds the canned soups, looking at the list in his hand, when Jerry Daniels and Tony come through the door. Tony looks a little spacey and he needs a shave, but when he smiles, like he's smiling now at Phyllis, his teeth are clean and white.

Pothead son-of-a-bitch.

Joseph's hands become fists around the handle of the cart. Roxanna is two years his senior; he was just fourteen the year that she and Tony were an item, away from home for the first time, spending the summer travelling the chuckwagon circuit, working for his uncle as an outrider. She's told him about her first kiss (Quinn, in the cloakroom of the Community Hall), her first slow dance (the DJ played Nazareth), the blind date her cousin set up for her when she was fifteen (the guy was shorter than she was and chewed stick after stick of Juicy Fruit), but she won't tell him why, all those years ago, she broke up with Tony Bryant.

"Jerry. Tony." He nods in the direction of the two men, who are now leaning against the pop cooler that sits beside the window, each with a can of Pepsi in his hand.

"Be right with you," Phyllis says to Joseph. She's in the middle of filling the high rack behind the counter with a new shipment of cigarettes.

"Know of anyone with a horse for sale?" Jerry asks.

Phyllis's elbow jostles the rack as she turns to pick up another carton. Packages of DuMaurier cascade onto the floor. Joseph moves to help her pick them up, kneeling behind the counter.

"Fuller usually has one or two," he says.

Straightening up, he sees Jerry alone against the cooler. His eyes move past the man to the window, and he sees Tony, outside now, standing a little apart from the women at the fruit truck.

"Fuller's too pricey," Jerry says. "I don't need a purebred."

Tony hooks a stack of two boxes under one arm, then looks sideways at Roxanna, eyebrows raised, his mouth shaped into a half-grin as he points to another box on the counter.

Joseph watches, his hands full of cigarette packs. Phyllis moves between him and the end of the counter, blocking his path. When he takes the groceries out to the truck, a box of peaches is in the back and Roxanna is already sitting in the cab.

On the way home, Joseph folds his jacket into a pillow for her. She lays her head on the seat next to his thigh and fiddles with the radio, finally settling for half-heard snatches of harmonica. He looks down at the side of her face, her open, unreadable eye, the red scarf, knotted at the nape of her neck, the red lipstick. The truck starts to slow as they begin the drive up Beaumont's hill. He looks ahead again, careful to stay on his own side of the road.

"About Tony —"

"I'm tired."

She's like the buried rocks he encounters once in a while when putting in the posts for a barbed wire fence. Easier to make a zigzag fence than try to unearth the stone.

Rows of drying plants hang in bunches from the rafters in Tony's attic. Early morning light enters in a single shaft from the dormer. Shingle flies buzz against the glass. Tony drops a seed head into a paper bag, folds down the top, shakes the bag until he can hear seeds rattling around inside, then transfers them to a plastic bag

Laney's pissed off. She heard him come home this morning, just before dawn, but she won't ask him where he's been. She's in the kitchen, canning peaches, immersing each fruit in boiling water before slipping it out of its skin.

Plot #6, September 3, 2000.

He labels every batch. Each plot has a number that follows the plants through drying and bagging. Once the plants from Plot #6 are completely dry, he'll crush, bag and label them. Now he's got two bags, one to smoke and one to plant. Sometime during the winter, he'll smoke Plot #6 and make a record of what the high is like. Come spring, he'll use the records to choose the seed he wants to grow. It's a precise system, Ganja's system, one he'd never have come up with on his own.

Trouble with you, Tony, the older man used to say, making marks in his notebook, trouble is, your mind works like a plant. The past is your ass-backwards sun, and what goes on in your head can't help turning toward that ass-backwards light.

Suzy Saretsky's father's dugout, the summer before grade twelve.

A bunch of them drinking, filling Styrofoam cups with tequila and Mountain Dew and calling the mix a margarita. Someone yells, not Tony, someone else, maybe Quinn or Winston.

Chicken fights.

They pile into the water. He looks for Roxanna in the shallow end of the dugout. She has a hand on Quinn's arm, so he grabs the girl closest to him, who happens to be Suzy, and hoists her onto his shoulders. Her thighs press against his neck, the softness of her crotch cradles the back of his head. His feet brace themselves against the bottom of the dugout. Caught up in the moment, laughing and shouting, he and Suzy topple all the others.

His towel is spread beside Roxanna's. She is there ahead of him, sleek with water, gleaming with it, small rivers running from the heavy wetness of her long hair. She turns away, ignores him, bends to pick up a towel.

He moves closer, presses his body against her back.

She takes a step away, brings the towel to her face, her neck. Starts drying her forearms, as if he doesn't exist.

"Hey," he says, and he grabs her gently by the hair. Still playing.

Her head jerks forward, away from his hand, and then it's not a game anymore, and he's angry, not irritated or confused but filled with a sudden and full-blown rage. He pulls harder, hard enough to hurt, winding the wet length around his fist, pressing his knuckles against her skull.

"Hey."

He steps forward, simultaneously exerting pressure so she has to turn her head and they are face to face. She looks through him, as if he is the surface, as if she is more interested in whatever crawls in the mud of the bottom than she is in him.

"Easy, Tony," Quinn says, moving toward them. "Ease up."

Quinn's hand is on his arm. The others stand still, except for Winston, who tosses a set of keys in a glittering arc toward Roxanna. She snatches them, one-handed, from the air and walks away, drives away in Winston's father's truck.

Joseph wakes and sees his wife entire; her back as she sits on the edge of the bed, the cotton of her shirt hanging in folds from the points of her shoulder blades and her front, her face reflected in the mirror on the dresser. New hair is starting to grow on her head, the way they said it would, right now just a dusting, like a dark shadow across her scalp. Joseph has grown used to her lack of hair and her visible bones, but the back of her neck still surprises him, lights in him a sharp, short-lived desire, as if the beauty of her diminished body has come to rest in that one part.

She is holding the red wild rag in her hands.

"Remember the time your uncle's chuckwagon won the fifty thousand?"

What a race. He rode the last stretch of track a second behind the wagon, the other outrider's horse flanking him, all the horses straining toward the end, everything going right, feeling right, their small world the luckiest place to live.

"You were wearing this." She folds the silk into a triangle and begins to tie it around her head. He sits up, shifts himself so his body fits behind hers. His fingers finish the knot.

"Why don't you lie down awhile? The kids are still sleeping."

She stretches out, fully dressed, and lets him cover her before he goes downstairs and out the door.

He almost misses it, the small bag left on his back step. Dew has beaded on the surface of the plastic, tiny drops of moisture, not enough to obscure the words written on the scrap of paper inside.

Plot #5. For Roxanna.

The bag contains dried bits of leaf and stem, not unlike the alfalfa hay he feeds the horses.

He looks at it another moment, then jams it into his pocket and heads toward the corral. Back in April, when he was making all those trips to the hospital with Roxanna, his brother Roland and some neighbours got together and did his work for him, sorted the calves, needled, dehorned and castrated them. He doesn't know who was doing the castrating, but whoever did it had used the Burdizzo instead of a knife, and the clamp missed a testicle.

The steer standing in the pen by the barn is a stag, his scrotum unbalanced, one side soft and empty, the other large and firm. Buyers don't want bull beef, so that missed testicle, if left alone, will cost at least two hundred dollars when the steer goes to market. He herds the animal toward the far side of the corral, where a gate opens to a narrow passage ending in a squeeze chute. The steer circles the corral once, then makes its way through the opening.

Joseph moves quickly, closing the gate. The animal trots forward until it's in the chute, and he pulls a lever, trapping the steer, tightening the sides against its body, making it hard for the animal to kick or buck. He reaches underneath its belly, leaning against the chute for balance, one hand finding the maturing nut, the other holding the scalpel. One clean cut opens the bottom of the scrotum. The animal expels a deep snort of pain and tries to buck. Joseph slides his fingers into the scrotum, hooks them around the slippery nut and pulls, stretching the connecting cord until it breaks somewhere high in the belly. The steer snorts again, then stands quiet. The testicle glistens, cupped in Joseph's palm. He wipes the blood from the knife on his pant leg, then slips the blade into his jacket pocket next to the bag of pot, still kneeling by the chute, still holding the steer's testicle in his other hand, unwilling to throw the severed flesh to the waiting cats. Immobilized and wondering what to do with it all.

As Near as Not

Jake takes off his shoes and socks before beginning to climb the ladder that leads to the top of the Eyehill grain elevator. The hot metal of the rungs stings the soles of his bare feet, but he feels little sensation in the palms of his hands, callused as they are from years of hard use. He climbs easily, moving smoothly up the silver wall. He's hauled his grain here since they built the new facility back in '79, and before that he'd hauled to the old Federal Grain. He's watched billions of kernels disappear into the grated bowels of their annexes. A thin barrier of wood and steel is all that separates him from the seed of tens of thousands of acres. He imagines the elevator wall bursting like a dam, releasing a golden tidal wave of wheat upon him. He would drown in it, like Jim Schmidt had drowned three years ago in his own grain bin, sucked beneath the surface of the wheat by the pull of the auger, suffocating in a quicksand of kernels. Jim had been careless. The man pulls himself slowly and deliberately up the ladder, hand over hand, rung by rung, his body moving with the repetitive rhythm of waves on a beach.

The boy passes one of his mother's slippery scarves to Manny.

"Tie that around your head."

He reaches into his pocket and pulls out a pair of gold hoop earrings with clasps at the back that snap onto the soft lobe with enough force to bring tears to the eyes of a weaker boy. Manny stares.

"We're pirates."

They stand on the deck of Manny's father's fishing boat. The old man isn't there to tell them not to waste their time and hand them a net full of knots to unsnarl. There are dozens of boats in the harbour of St. Anne's Bay, fat and colourful, reeling slightly in the gentle waves the way the men who skippered them reeled home from the pub on a Friday night. There is seaweed on the shore, first wet and slimy, then dry and brittle. It catches in the rocks and undulates in the waves like ribbons. The air is sharp with the smell of salt and dead cod. His mother would have him by the neck if she knew about the scarves, but when he left the house she hadn't even noticed. She was at the kitchen table, writing a letter. Before sealing it in the envelope, she sprayed perfume into the air and waved the paper back and forth through the fine mist. He left quickly, before any of the sweetness had a chance to settle on his skin.

The dry heat of the sun reflected from the elevator's surface burns the inside of Jake's nose as he breathes, in and out, in and out, same rhythm as the water that lapped the shores of St. Anne's. He removes one hand from the rungs, and for a moment his weight hangs suspended, connected to the ladder by only one hand above his head and his feet on the rung beneath. He squints at the fields below. Those to the north are dotted with oil wells, the barley planted around the leases turned prematurely gold by drought, the heads bleached white on the tops of hills where the soil is thinner. A haze of dust blurs the outlines of buildings on the edges of town. Eyehill on a Sunday afternoon. Peeled paint, long grass and cracked windows tell the story of families gone; the houses like old people napping, dozing in and out of dreams peopled by chil-

dren who moved to the city. A grey dust speck of cat sleeps on
the front step of the post office, where three times a week Jake
picks up the mail. Three days ago, he opened his mail box and
found the notice from the bank sandwiched between the fertilizer bill and an invitation to the wedding of a neighbour's
son. Possibility of foreclosure. He brings his free hand to his
chest and touches the pocket of his workshirt, hears the slight
crackle of the envelope that lies between his hand and his heart.
He has not shown it to anyone. His gaze drifts downward
again to the white building that is the post office. It looks tiny
and less ominous from above.

"So you're the boy."

The man who helped his mother down from the train now
turns to look at him. He is older than Manny's father, with grey
hair that sticks out from under his hat and glasses that sit
crooked on his face. Jake looks past him at the shining rows of
strange triangular metal pieces that some men are unloading
from the train. His mother picks up her small travelling bag and
takes a step or two to the left, which moves her away from
Jake's side and closer to the man. The man takes the bag from
her. Jake struggles with one of their heavy suitcases.

The man watches, then shifts the small bag under his arm to
free both hands, takes the suitcase from Jake with one and picks
up a second suitcase with the other. When they pass the rows of
metal pieces, he pauses and jerks his head in that direction.

"Cultivator shovels," he says.

They move on, toward the man's truck.

"Would you like to ride in the back?" he asks, hefting the
suitcases over the side.

Jake nods and climbs in, settling into a space between the
two large suitcases, his back pressed against the end of the box
closest to the truck's cab. His first experience of the prairie: a

rush of wind and sky, twin trails of dust kicked up by the tires, and the sensation of leaving part of his gut behind as the truck rises and falls on the backs of the short sharp hills.

The arid stillness below stirs up in him an old, sudden home-sickness for the sea, as sharp a longing as the one he'd felt as a boy when his mother moved him to the prairie so she could marry Burnell MacInnes. The dry air had made him thirsty all the time. The dust rising from behind the cabless tractor coated his throat and filled his lungs. The thirst and the homesickness lessened as he grew, but his longing for the bay did not leave him until he met Judy. They married when he was nineteen. She had been seventeen. She admired his large hands, already roughened by work but possessing a gentleness learned from untangling fishing nets. She liked the way he spoke, his words still touched with the rhythm of the East. She loved him because of this, but also because of the fields that Burnell MacInnes's father had carved out of the prairie. All her people were farm-ers. He doubts she would have married a man who made his living on a boat.

He turns away from the sight of his wheat field in the dis-tance, each plump kernel shrivelling as the sun sucked the milky juice from its centre, leaving it to rattle, wrinkled and old, in its useless blanket of husk. He reaches for the next rung with his free hand and tilts his head back, looking upwards, ascending more slowly now, his palms becoming slippery with sweat. He stops to wipe his hands on the front of his shirt and leans against the ladder, feeling the rungs like burning bands against his legs. He thinks of sea water, salt on his lips that is not the sweat of his body. His memory of childhood is a fishnet full of silvery, writhing images. The storms and the stuff that washed up on shore afterward, big square timbers, bits of rope, trees with roots like arthritic fingers, and once a pocket watch that could still be wound. Sun striking the window glass of the small house where his mother lived with her mother until the old lady died and was buried in the churchyard, not far from the place where the giant marble headstone of the man who once owned a dozen sailing ships cast its shadow on the grass. The cliffs where he and Manny had dared each other to jump into the sea, its icy blueness, the shock of it, the fierce tingling as his skin spoke to him in a million voices, telling him he was alive.

The boy walked with the man behind the plow because his mother was gone and there was no other place. The noise of the world was insects humming and the swish of horses' tails and the scrape of a metal blade against stone. Sometimes, when the plow fetched up against things hidden underground, the boy heard the joints of the man's body creak and pop. The horses strained and grunted with the man until the thing beneath them gave way, and once again the earth furrowed softly, folding like a sheet of heavy cloth. The world was mostly sound and earth and the man's legs in front of him. The boy kept his eyes to the ground, watching for treasures the earth might show forth, and because the furrows were deep and it was easy to fall. Small bright stones. Worms. The sod turned over, opening in a way that made him think of his mother's hands. He remembered a time when she'd called him from his play, her hands closed one over the other like a box with a lid. Slowly, she'd knelt down beside him and opened her hands. A strange white moth with feathered antennae and a large spot of green on each wing quivered in her palm.

The boy particularly hoped to find arrowheads. They were there, hidden under the roots of grass. He'd found three already. One was very small, no bigger than the man's thumbnail. For killing birds, the man said. The boy remembered everything the man said, because the man spoke so seldom. He pointed or nodded or lifted his chin. These signals were understood by the boy. Hurry up. Fetch the water. Bring more wood.

The boy nearly ran into the legs in front of him. The man had stopped. There was a scattered pile of rocks in front of the horses, stones of all sizes, one of which was particularly large. It came level with the man's shoulders. The man left the plow, walked over to the large rock and laid his hand on it. He jerked his head to indicate the boy should do the same. The stone was warm from the sun and rough with patches of orange.

"Lichens," the man said, rubbing a thumb over one of the orange spots.

Lichens. The boy thought the word.

"This pile of stones once meant something to somebody," the man said. "They were put here for a reason, by others before us. They are not to be moved. No MacInnes will ever move them."

The man went back to the plow. The boy thought, those stones are for a reason. They are not to be moved. Lichen is the orange patch on a rock. Small arrowheads are for killing birds. The man clicked his tongue and moved the reins, so that the horses turned aside. No stones were dislodged by the blade. Earth turned over.

This is the story Burnell MacInnes tells Jake when Jake is seventeen. He has to stop a couple of times in the middle of telling it because parts of him are wearing out. Maybe his heart, maybe his lungs, maybe both. The doctor can't say for sure.

"Remember," he says, "you're as near to MacInnes as not."

He rests his hand, for just a moment, on Jake's shoulder, and Jake, who has grown fond of his stepfather, stands quietly beneath the weight of it.

He is very high now, perhaps only twenty feet from the top of the elevator. Surrounded by sky on three sides, he feels cooler somehow, enveloped in blue. There is a slight breeze like the

one he remembered from long-ago mornings on the deck of
Manny's father's boat, but there are no gulls and that seems
strange. The town beneath him appears unoccupied, no one
driving down Main Street who might notice a man on top of
an elevator and be curious about his presence there. He climbs
the remaining distance and pulls himself onto the roof. A pale,
frothy line of cloud disturbs the surface of the sky where a jet
churns a white wake as it travels eastward.

He stops to rest. Heat and height combine to make him
dizzy. He looks at his watch. Judy will be peeling potatoes as
she looks out the west window above the sink.

If you could live anywhere you wanted, Judy, where would
it be?

He remembers how she looked up from where she sat in the
shade of the north wall of the house. A half-full bowl of peas,
picked in the cool of dawn while the pods still had some snap,
rested on her lap. The dog lay content beside her. She laughed.

You know I don't even like to go to town for groceries.

Anywhere. Where would it be?

Right where I am, Jake. Just where I am.

She expects him home for supper, just as she expects to
harvest this fall and plant again next spring. He does not look
down. He takes off his watch and lays it carefully on the roof,
not wanting to scratch the crystal. He unbuttons his red workshirt and lets the air touch his skin. He looks at his torso and
his arms in the half-anxious, half-admiring manner of a twelve-
year-old boy. His stomach is flat for a man his age, and his arm
muscles create a satisfying bulge between elbow and shoulder.
He pauses, thinking of potatoes boiling away the minutes and
the woman waiting for him to come home before she puts the
rest of the vegetables on to cook. He makes a movement toward
the ladder, bending slightly and indecisively, as if considering
descent, but the fields below tilt, and his distant farm seems to
rise toward him in the smothering heat. His vision blurs slight-

ly, and he almost loses his balance, nearly topples gracelessly downward. He steps back and closes his eyes, seeing empty fields, an empty kitchen.

Hot again. All he wants to do is swim, to cool himself. He steps up to the edge of the rooftop, ignoring the pain as it burns the skin on the bottom of his feet. He removes his shirt completely and throws it into the air, letting it sink and disappear. His toes curl, gripping the strange smooth metal of the roof, so different from the rocks of the sea cliffs. He thinks of Manny daring him to dive from the highest rocks. His stomach tightens with a childish, half-fearful anticipation. He breathes deeply, eyes closed, knees bent, swinging his arms a few times, testing the dangerous way the momentum might carry him forward. Below, his shirt hangs caught in the branches of a tree, one sleeve undulating like frayed seaweed caught in a gentle current.

Coyote Pietà

Nothing's so bad that it can't get worse. That's what my father always says, and he sticks to it. When I was thirteen, I thought I'd put him to the test, and I asked, What about my mother leaving you with a three-year-old kid to raise by yourself? He didn't flinch. Well, he said, in that slow way of his, she could have taken you with her.

Which, of course, leaves me wondering. Why didn't she?

Anyway, some good did come of it. One day my father opened the door and Roxanna stood on the step, holding a small blue suitcase. Inside were two Barbie dolls and the clothes to dress them in, a package of Juicy Fruit gum (just one of the many things we never told my father about, because I wasn't supposed to have gum; he said if I swallowed it, it would take seven years to digest), a brush and a comb, and a *Seventeen* magazine, which I was not allowed to touch because I was not seventeen (I was only six). She was not seventeen either. She was going into grade seven, and my father had made arrangements with Roxanna's mother for her to stay with me that summer so I would not have to spend all day in the cab of the tractor, going round and round the fields with him, a child-care strategy that he minded more than I did.

Roxanna and I spent much of those two months sitting in front of the television, she on the couch, me on the floor, the back of my head resting on the upholstery between her knees. She wasn't a talker. She combed my hair in silence, braided it into a crown around my head, combed it smooth, pinned it into a French roll, combed it out again. We played cards, mostly blind thirty-one, and she was lucky with the discards.

She stayed with me every summer after that, and as the years went on and she got old enough to work after school, she came in for a few hours every day to clean the house and make supper for my father and me. She continued to do this after she married Joseph Lafonde, even though I could cook a little. She taught me how to numb the skin of my eyebrows with an ice cube before plucking, how to put a drop of clear nail polish on a stocking to stop a run, and how to make my nose look smaller by applying a dot of concealer to the bridge. And, on the afternoon before I went on my first blind date (Carmela's cousin Emmet, from Saskatoon), she taught me how to keep a boy from touching my breasts.

"Emmet isn't a very promising name," she said. "The old guy who lived in the shack by the tracks, his name was Emmet. He poisoned himself by burning railway ties in his wood stove. The fumes from the creosote got him."

She moved to stand in front of me, close, maybe six inches away. "Okay, if he's kissing you, his hands will probably start at your waist. Now, don't get the wrong idea, this is just a demonstration."

"He's not going to kiss me. He doesn't even know me."

She gave me a look — are you an idiot, or what? — and rested her hands on either side of my waist.

"Okay, once he's got this far, he might try something like this." She moved her hand up, along the rib cage, towards my breast, then she paused. "At first, you want to be polite. Bend your elbow and clamp your arm tight to your side."

I clamped.

She tried to slide her hand further up and couldn't do it, proving that my arm would create an effective barrier.

"See," she said, "now he can't get where he's going, you

don't have to say a word, he knows what kind of girl you are, and nobody has to be embarrassed."

She dropped her hands and stepped away.

"If he doesn't back off, forget being polite. Give him the knee."

"The knee?"

"I mean it, Rhea. Right in the crotch. Sometimes it's the only thing they understand."

I'd have liked to give Thomas the knee after he had sex with that hitchhiker (it was my back seat, my car that took him on his little pilgrimage, the same car that picked her up). What I did instead was drive away from the shrine of Our Lady of Sorrows, leaving the two of them open-mouthed and gawking at the sight of my tail lights disappearing down the road. I'd still like to give Jarvis the knee for being stupid enough to have sex with Carmela without using a condom and then asking my father to tell me she was pregnant, rather than telling me himself. But my father? I've forgiven him and we're speaking again, the whole business of stopping for the hitchhiker having taught me that you can't predict the consequences of doing someone else a favour.

"Rhea?" My father, shouting into the phone. The new phone the company installed has never worked properly. My father called to have it repaired twice, and twice the repairmen got lost on the winding gravel roads. The line breaks into static for a moment, then his voice comes through.

"Rhea. Just wanted to tell you something. They're having a benefit dance" — static, then he's back — "wants to take her to a clinic in Mexico."

"What?"

"Some special breast cancer clinic."

"Who has cancer?"

The line starts to break up again.

"Roxanna. Since last spring. Didn't I tell you?"

I can't answer. It's like the time I watched Jarvis lose his footing on the tree branch and start falling, ricocheting between the branches like the shot in the pinball machine that sits in the lobby of the Eyehill Hotel. I want to yell No or Stop, nothing fancy, just a simple negative, but nothing comes out of my mouth.

"Damn phone," I hear my father saying, then there is a loud thunk as he bangs the receiver against the arm of his chair. "Rhea? Are you there?"

"When is it?"

"Three weeks from Saturday."

The phone goes from bad to worse, crackling, sputtering, gaps of dead air stretching longer, until finally he's gone and I'm left with the one word that made itself clear in that last minute or two of static. Should. He was probably saying, Rhea, you should come back.

Let's say I go back to Eyehill because of Roxanna and sit through an evening where, at some point, I'm sure to come face to face with Jarvis and Carmela (she used to practice writing her name on her algebra binder as if they were married, Carmela Marie McGowan, and now, of course, they are). I'll have to speak to the two of them, offer my congratulations, admire the ring, hold the child if it's offered. Let's say God is watching, pen in hand, keeping track. My going back should be worth a lot of marks in Roxanna's column. It should count for something.

I can still see Roxanna frying sausages. She smokes cigarettes in the house without my father knowing, using a china pickle dish for an ashtray and never leaving the tiniest smudge of evidence behind her. She wets her hand under the tap and shakes her fingers over the cast iron frying pan on the stove. The water instantly sizzles into steam. That's how you know it's ready, she says, sliding a gob of lard into the pan. The light in the kitchen grows dim from the smoke of grease and cigarettes. It is the right time of day, just as the sun is going down, and the right kind of light. If I'm in the kitchen while Roxanna is cooking, she will tell me Eyehill stories.

"Walter Saretsky and Jerry Daniels got ino a fight on Main Street last night," she says, adjusting the lid on the potato pot so steam can escape. "It started in the beer parlour, after Jerry won three games of pool in a row. Then he put some money in the jukebox and hit the button for a song that Saretsky took exception to" — she stops to take in a lungful of cigarette — "then there were words exchanged, and Jerry called Saretsky a c-sucker, and that really heated things up."

She pauses to stir the sausages.

"They took Jerry to the hospital. Twenty-seven stitches, but the dentist they called in saved his teeth. Everyone's saying Saretsky hit Jerry all out of proportion to what he said. They say the truth is that Jerry is sleeping with Saretsky's wife. Joseph heard rumours it's worse than that. He heard that Jerry was sleeping with Suzy."

Suzy is the daughter, same age as Roxanna. Not quite nineteen.

"Imagine," she says, "him old enough to be her father." She stops what she's doing and looks straight at me, half-squinting the way she does when she's going to say something important.

"You stay away from Jerry. Maybe Suzy's the type to go looking for it, but you stay away all the same." She attacks the sausages with the lifter, stirring up a smoke and sizzle.

"Men think with their peckers, Rhea." She stops stirring for a moment and adds, "Don't tell your father I said pecker."

The next day, I pass again through the group of girls that congregates in the washroom to share combs and lip gloss and sticks of breath-freshening gum. An awkward situation, because I have always chosen to spend most of my recess time with the boys, playing soccer and can-can and five hundred while the girls cluster on the school steps. Problem now is, the boys (Jarvis too) are starting to drift over to those steps, to hang around just outside the circle of girls and vie for their attention. Yesterday, Jarvis lobbed snowballs toward the principal's car. Carmela squealed and laid a hand on his jacket to stop him. Be careful, Jarvis, another girl said, and the next snowball splattered against an upstairs window, startling the three teachers that sat drinking coffee in the lounge. The principal stuck his head out and said, "Was that you, McGowan?" But Jarvis was gone.

I step out of the washroom stall. School won't start for another ten minutes. The girls are whispering, but loud enough that I can hear, and the topic of their conversation is Suzy Saretsky.

"I heard my mom say they better do something with her fast or you-know-what will happen," says Carmela.

"What?" Christy asks.

The rest giggle and roll their eyes. I walk to the sink, which brings me closer to them, and I hear Sherry pick it up from there. "My mom can't get over it. She said what's wrong with Jerry, him with a pretty wife who always keeps herself done up nice?"

The rest of the girls consider this in silence. I see my chance and I take it.

"Men think with their peckers," I say.

They all stare.

Then Carmela starts to laugh. The others join in. She stops to catch her breath.

"How true," she says, and the others nod as if they knew it all along.

The circle widens just a bit to include me. I have to stand with one shoulder behind Christy, but I'm in.

———

God's Odds and Ends. That's the name of the shop where I've been working since I quit waitressing at the Athena. The woman who hired me was a regular customer at the restaurant, and one day, about eighteen months ago, after I got back from that disastrous road trip with Thomas, she and another woman came in for the lunch special. Just as I was gathering up the dirty dishes, she stopped to stare at me for a minute.

"My friend here thinks you have a lovely pink aura," she said.

Lesbians. Just what I need.

"It's a little dull around the edges," the friend said, "but some meditation would polish it right up."

The other woman explained, "I own a shop not far from here. I'm looking to hire, but I need someone who's trustworthy. Pink is a good sign, but I'd like additional references. Drop by if you're interested."

So I did, and now she's talking about me working my way into a partnership. At God's Odds — that's what I call it, more because of the clientele than the merchandise — we sell New Age stuff: incense, crystals, magnets, that sort of thing, but the bread and butter of the business is still Christian: books, audio tapes, gifts (you can even buy religious pot holders), and a lot of Catholic paraphernalia. We have a rack of rosaries.

I'd just started cleaning some of the crystals on display when this bald guy walks in with a brown envelope under his arm.

"Rhea?" He runs his hand up over his eyes and across the smooth surface of his scalp.

I look down at the piece of cotton rag in my hand, as if my polishing had conjured him up like a genie from a bottle.

"Thomas." It takes me a second to recognize him because he's shaved his head.

He asks me how long I've worked at the store, tells me he dropped his Latin classes but has been studying privately for over a year with one of the brothers at the seminary. He says he can't eat Greek anymore, it reminds him too much of me.

A Sunday school teacher comes in. "Do you sell stickers?" she asks.

I show her a shelf full of happy faces, crosses, Jesus Loves Me. I drift back over to the counter where Thomas is waiting.

"The business with the hitchhiker," he half-whispers. "It meant nothing."

The woman comes to the till with a sheaf of sticker sheets. She's maybe forty-five or fifty, not too many wrinkles, hair streaked, good makeup. She's wearing a big diamond engagement ring and a matching wedding band. She teaches Sunday school; she must know something about judgment. I want to ask her, Is a man who can have meaningless sex more attractive than a man who is unfaithful? But she turns away toward the display of children's books, leaving the stickers on the counter.

"So, what are you looking for these days, Thomas?"

He pulls a sheet of paper out of the envelope and hands it to me. It's a picture of what is supposed to be a statue of one person holding another, but it isn't finished. The stone is scratched and pitted with chisel marks. The person behind supports the sagging body of the person in front, and while the person being held is obviously male (he has a beard), the sex of the one in the back is harder to determine. It's probably a woman, because of the way her head and body are cloaked. The features of the face, especially from the nose down, are too unformed to be either male or female, but none of that matters. What catches me is the expression on that face, the mixture of sorrow and love that seems to radiate from the stone, so intense it doesn't need eyebrows or nostrils or even the slight bulge of flesh that marks where a lip might curve up or down.

"Mary grieving over the dead Christ," Thomas says. "Michelangelo worked on this last Pietà until a few days before he died, then he tried to destroy it."

I catch myself leaning closer to him. I'm about to ask why, why would someone destroy something that showed so much promise? But I stop, pull back a little. This picture, the story behind it, so different from the Eyehill stories of my childhood, these are the lures that Thomas dangles in front of me.

He continues, "I'm looking for a small copy of this sculpture, something that would sit on a desk or a shelf, not as small as a paperweight, but not too big either."

"I'll need to keep the picture. Check some catalogues." He nods, and I grab a pen to write down a few details on the bottom of the paper. "How do you spell pietà?"

"P-i-e-t-a. Italian word for pity." He stands for a minute, watching me write, then he asks, "Would you like to go for coffee?"

"I'm not taking a break today."

"What about this weekend?"

"I'm going away." He raises his eyebrows at me. "Really, I am. I'm going to Eyehill."

The Sunday school woman returns to the counter with books to add to her pile of stickers.

"I'll come back," he says.

I ring in the woman's stuff, bag it, smile, bend down to look for a quarter I dropped, and by the time I straighten up, they are both gone. I look down at Thomas's paper, at the face of the woman, at the word written beneath it.

Our grade four teacher always said a picture's worth a thousand words, as he passed out the scissors and the construction paper for yet another collage, and he was right. Pity. Too weak a word, because whatever the woman is feeling, it's strong enough to reach out and grab you by the throat. I know about pity. It tiptoes and whispers and looks out of the corner of an eye, and it was always part of the Eyehill story that was mine.

Poor Rhea.

Living out on that farm, pretty much raising herself. A girl that age needs her mother.

I hear Roxanna still goes there most days.

Kind of an odd set-up, a nice-looking girl like Roxanna bothering with Al Jardine's kid.

Saw her car there the other day. Two o'clock. Plenty of time before school's out.

Al's wife's gone. There's lots worse for the girl than Roxanna.

Helen Jardine will come back when her fancy city man gets tired of her.

When she runs out of money.

When she gets out of jail.

Al would be soft in the head to take her back.

You ever see Helen in a tight sweater? His head would be the only soft part of him.

Shh. Rhea might hear.

Last customer of the day rolls in five minutes before closing time. She's dressed up, black dress, black patent sandals, three shades of eyeshadow blended on her lids. I've packed an overnight bag and filled the car with gas. I want to get to the Eyehill Community Hall early so I can pick a seat with my back to the wall. I can tell by looking at her: this woman is going to make me late.

She goes over to the wall where the jewellery is displayed, ignores the gold crosses and begins to pick up various crystal pendants, holding each up to the mirror.

"Are you looking for something special?" A stupid question, all the people who shop New Age are looking for something special, but the owner requires staff to ask it. She chooses a blue-tinted stone and turns to me.

"What's this one mean?"

"That's part of our Serenity line. Very popular."

"Not what I need."

She plucks another chain, holds it so the crystal rests just above her cleavage.

"I have a date tonight," she says, "with a man who is five years younger. My husband doesn't know."

What is it that makes these people think a clerk who rings up their purchases in a store like God's Odds is the next thing to a priest? Just the other day, a woman comes in here and buys a small, egg-shaped stone. As I'm wrapping it in tissue paper, she says, I had an abortion a few weeks ago. I just couldn't be pregnant. I'm in the last year of my degree. As I slipped the bundle into a little bag, she said, I'm going to bury this stone in the garden, and then she handed me a twenty.

"That would be a good choice," I say to the woman in black. "That type of crystal is great for channelling positive energy."

"I need all the energy I can get," the woman says, tucking the stone into her palm, but she still has to look at all the others in the display before finally letting me ring it up. The traffic downtown is terrible (Christmas shopping is in full swing), and I'm terrible at weaving my way through it. Then, an hour out of the city, I'm held up by a train at a highway crossing.

Two hours later, by the time the lights of Eyehill come into view, it's nine o'clock. I turn just before town, drive up the dirt road that will take me past the McGowans' farm, past the original Lafonde homestead, with its tiny abandoned house where Émile and his wife first lived. Pockets of willow and the dead brown stalks of yellow clover poke their way up through the glitter of snow that has collected in the ditches.

On the next hill, I can see the yard light my father has switched on for me. The road slopes down, then up, then down again, the rise and fall a familiar rhythm. The white shapes of the Charolais cattle in my father's herd press themselves against the fence. It's too dark to see other things I know are there beyond them: the furrows made by cultivator blades in the summerfallow, the deer wintering in the shelter of the poplar bluffs, the hilltop, the coyote who lopes down the other side of it and crawls under the fence that separates Jardine land from McGowan land, startling a string of horses, the spring where, in warmer weather, those horses drink, the water seeping from the earth to lie stagnant in a pasture hollow, bubbles rising from the mud bottom now frozen in place.

I pull into the yard and knock on the door, but there is no answer. Inside, the smell of the house envelopes me, still faintly medicinal (cow remedies, the vaccines and antibiotics in the brown, rubber-topped bottles), layered with toasted bread (my father's specialty, the BLT), and cellar dirt and the strong green soap he uses to wash his hands. My father isn't in the kitchen. I go through another door, into the living room, following the sound of the hockey game on TV.

He's fallen asleep in the recliner, a folded copy of *The Western Producer* on his chest. It's been nearly four years since I've seen him, and I could cry, the tears brought on not so much by the sight of his face as by his feet, tipped up so the bottoms of his socks are visible. In my mind, he is always booted: soft leather cowboy boots with a roper's heel, steel-toed work boots for the carpentry work he did on the side. There's a tightness in my throat, a pain. Not good. I haven't even made it to the dance yet.

Roxanna always said it never hurts to do your hair. So I leave him sleeping and dig my curling iron out of the overnight bag. I plug it in near the medicine chest mirror that hangs above the sink. I think of waitressing and taking a class at the university and driving across Canada and selling crystals, all I've done that a lot of people in Eyehill have never done and never will do. I think of Thomas and his obsessions, his desire to have a vision of the Blessed Virgin.

I touch up my bangs and open the medicine cabinet to look for an Aspirin, the tight pain in my throat having travelled to my head, settling in just behind my left eye. In the corner of the bottom shelf, there's a short round bottle of perfume, almost empty. It's been there for years, as long as I can remember. It must have been my mother's. I find the Aspirin, shake a pill out of the bottle.

"Rhea."

The voice startles me. My father stands in the doorway between the living room and the kitchen, wearing his dress clothes. I put the pill bottle next to the perfume on the shelf and step toward him, a man who doesn't care if he ever sees the Mother of God, but who has never quite given up the hope that if he stays right where she left him, he might see his wife one more time.

When we walk into the little porch whose double doors are the entry into the bigger space of the Community Hall, the first person I see is Carmela. She faces the doors, but her eyes look down at the little girl in front of her. They are holding hands, and she is swinging the girl's arms to the beat of the music. The child wears a red dress, and short ringlets of fine hair brush the back of the collar. I turn away to follow my father into the cloakroom.

The band on the stage is local. Billy Warzecka and the Midnight Coyote. Three old men: one with an accordion, another with a fiddle, and a lead singer who plays guitar. The tunes haven't changed: "Beer Barrel Polka," "Tennessee Waltz," "Counting Flowers on the Wall." One of the men (I can't remember which) is called the Midnight Coyote, because the band makes a point of playing their wildest polka right before midnight, and at the end of the song, the man throws back his head and howls like a coyote, inviting the dancers to join in.

I'm out of the cloakroom just as the song is ending. Carmela waves a hand, and turns the little girl in a final half-circle so that the two of them are looking toward the door. The girl's face is disfigured by a large, purplish-red mark that encompasses the top of her left cheek, her left eye and a good part of her forehead. My father has moved forward to join a group of men standing near the bar. Carmela moves toward me, bringing the child with her.

"Rhea," she says. "Long time no see."

The little girl turns her face toward her mother's leg.

"Shy," she says. "Don't know where that came from. Certainly not from me." She drops a hand to the top of her daughter's head. "Emily, say hello to Mommy's friend."

The little girl looks at me. She has another purple mark on her neck, smaller, about the size of a quarter. After a second, she turns her head again, this time toward the wall, where Carmela's mother sits with some of the neighbours. The older woman holds out her arms for the child, and the little girl runs toward them. I'm trying to think of something to say to Carmela when a cold hand curves its fingers around my arm, and pulls me a quarter turn away from the other woman.

Roxanna, rescuing me.

"You cut your hair," she says. "Looks good."

I'd like to put my arms around her but she's not the hugging type, and neither am I, for that matter.

"You too," I say.

"Ha."

We move off to the side a little. Quinn arrives, holding hands with a woman I've never seen before.

"One of Eyehill's great love stories," Roxanna whispers. "Not long after you left. Just at the time when everyone thought he'd always be a bachelor, he meets her at the bank. She was dating a lawyer, but she left him to marry Quinn."

My friend Roland steps out from behind the bar where he's been serving drinks and makes his way toward us. Then it seems that everyone is there, clustered around me: Roland and his new girlfriend, my old 4-H leader and his wife, the guy who drove the school bus, and I'm telling them a funny story about one of the customers at God's Odds, and then I'm pulled toward the bar, and then Billy Warzecka plays a slow song and Roxanna (so, so thin) is dancing with Joseph. Just before Roland's girlfriend pulls him onto the dance floor, he leans over and whispers.

"Jarvis will be here later. He had to wait for a truck to come pick up his calves."

I'm left alone with Carmela.

"Where have you been all this time, Rhea? There was talk when you left that you'd found your mother and gone to live with her."

"I've got my own apartment."

She's drinking a glass of Sprite, plain, and I saw the raised eyebrows when she ordered it.

"I'm not taking any chances," she says, "not this time." She looks across the room to where her daughter sits, cuddled and almost asleep in her grandmother's arms. "When we took her to the city, the neurologist told us that some kids with port wine stain were slower than other children."

She takes another sip of the Sprite. "This baby's going to be different."

Myra Lafonde comes over and says it's time to organize the food, then she adds, "I just saw Jarvis come in."

"The pickles," I say. "I forgot the pickles in the truck."

"Stay here where it's warm," Myra says. "We've got plenty,"

But I can't wait to get out, keeping my eyes down, not wanting to see Jarvis or have him see me. I slide out one of the side exits, the same one I used the night we painted our initials on the bottom of the railway car, as eager now to sneak away from Jarvis as I was to sneak toward him then.

The pickles are right there on the seat. I pick them up, and the side of the glass jar seems to freeze to my hand, it's that cold. Still, I take the long way back. I walk past the buildings — the Municipal Office, the boarded-up garage, the Eyehill Hotel — all in darkness except for the hotel, where one illuminated window shows the man who keeps the bar sitting alone, watching television. Some people have started their cars to warm them up, and exhaust fogs the air. Red Christmas lights shine from the window of the Co-op. The music gets louder as I get closer. I stop for a minute in the shadow of the narrow space between the grocery store and the hotel.

The concrete steps that lead to the front door of the hall are sheltered by a little roof that juts from the wall above them. The roof is wired with a bulb that casts a circular pool of light. A man steps from inside the hall into the bright circle.

Jarvis.

He pauses on the step to adjust the coat wrapped around the sleeping child he carries in his arms, looks down at her disfigured face for a second, then up again, his own features simplified by shadow and distance and a fierce sort of heart-broken love. Behind him, in the big warm room, Joseph Lafonde takes Roxanna's arm. Al Jardine scans the crowd, searching for his missing daughter. It must be nearly time to go home, because inside the hall the music stops and the Midnight Coyote begins to howl.

They Secretly Hope for Rain

Unfortunately, his hands are not on her breasts. One rests on the soft hair of his chest and the other is concealed by the blue cotton roses of the top sheet. Quinn is sleeping, fell asleep almost instantly after he showered and ate.

Maggie sits up, blue roses dropping from her shoulders and breasts to reveal futile nakedness. It is harvest, and outside the bedroom, the earth spills its seed with shameless abundance. Her husband is not so generous. He sleeps, exhausted by the harvest, made a eunuch by the land. They are all like this in September: Myra's husband, Judy's husband, even the young and beautiful Genevieve's husband. The men don't know it, but the women discuss this on the phone. None of them have had sex for at least three weeks. Their husbands are too busy or too tired from working in the fields, but the women are not jealous of the land. The women do not resent the smell of grain dust on their men's clothing the way they would the perfume of a mistress because they are agreed that the earth is not female, despite the earnest mother earth imagery used by the inexperienced poets published in the Environment section of the *Star-Phoenix*. They laugh gently at the comparisons.

The women know that for a season at least, the earth is male. A polygamous male, a sultan, in fact. Myra, who has been spending her restless nights with steamy romance novels, suggested this. Maggie agrees. The men are willing slaves to the sultan. She and Myra discuss what it is like to be in a harem, to wait weeks, even months for one night of sex. The women listen to the weather forecasts, and while the men dutifully pray for sun, they secretly hope for rain.

She loves Quinn's hands. The cracks in them are permanently darkened with machine oil and dirt. This does not come off on her skin when he touches her, does not leave pale smudges across the slope of her breasts or a telltale line along her thigh. They are considerate hands. She imagines them in winter, ungloved, searching all the secret places where her pleasure hides. She leans over and kisses one of his knuckles, but he does not wake up. The nipple of one breast brushes against the fine hair on his arm. She stops breathing, tries to hold onto the sharp, sweet tingle, fearing the pleasure will be exhaled with her breath. The window is open, and a tiny breeze, like a fingernail pulled lightly across her skin, makes her aware of the surrounding air. Another gentle gust, insistent, wraps tendrils around her flesh, caressing like fingers.

She gets out of bed carelessly, purposely rocking the mattress, but her husband's eyes are still closed, and his breath comes in soft, regular half-snores. The sheet lies flat across his thighs. No blue roses spring to life. She turns away, resigned, and walks toward the open window, enjoying the shivers feathering over her nakedness. She listens. There is a murmur outside the window, a beckoning sound. The soft, shy place between her thighs becomes fierce. Her own fingers reach down to stroke, to soothe the restlessness. The wind is warm as breath on her breasts. As the beckoning grows louder, she stills her hand, straining to hear the sound. The wind again, rustling through the wheat field beneath the bedroom window; the field sounds like a lover, like soft sighs and sheets tangling, like a whisper on her bare shoulder.

Her robe is hanging on the bedroom door. She wouldn't think of going outdoors without covering herself, even though her closest neighbours live nearly two miles away, and the road by the house has been quiet for over an hour. She slips on the robe and ties it loosely before leaving the house. She uses the back door and does not turn on any lights. There is a quarter-moon that lights the way. Barefoot, she walks quickly to the field, her feet sinking slightly into the soft soil that has been abraded and revealed by tractor tires. At the edge of the field she unties the robe and lets the wind part it, lets the wind blow against her and lift the hair from her neck. At its urging, she allows the robe to fall into the dirt. Her breasts look large in the moonlight, and her body seems to have a thousand places to hide its pleasure. Dark places under arms, beneath nipples, in hollows of elbows and knees, between toes and fingers. She is more shadow than surface.

Short of breath as a girl held close in her first slow dance, she steps into the field of grain. The stalks of wheat reach almost to her breasts. The leaves and stems caress her, brushing lightly against skin, sliding between her legs as she walks forward. Each step is pleasure. She feels a heat within her like the sun on her back when she weeds the garden, a pleasant warmth that prom-ises burning, yet she is cool where the night air meets the slight wetness in the shadowed place between her legs. Exciting, contradictory sensations. She feels enveloped by the wind and the wheat, feels the seed against her thighs. Eagerly, she arches her back to take the pleasure, offering herself to the field while her husband sleeps.

A week later, it rains. The morning after the first rainy night, her husband looks at the robe covering the breasts he has touched and sees a faint smudge of dirt on the lapel. He resolves to use more soap when he washes his hands. Myra and Judy, who are more careful housekeepers, wash their bathrobes twice a week in September. Genevieve has no robe to wash. When the men go to town to run wet-weather errands, the women share laundry secrets over the phone.

Another Man's Dog

Roland Lafonde watches while his three-year-old sleeps. The boy lies on his back, his left eye closed in sleep, his right eye heavily bandaged, the gash that runs from chin to ear neatly sewn shut, the skin surrounding it still slightly yellow from the antiseptic. The bedroom door is open a crack, and Roland can hear the sound of plates being set one on top of the other as his wife unloads the dishwasher. He reaches a finger out to touch the back of his boy's hand. The child twitches a little. A telephone rings in another part of the house, and the sound of Genevieve's voice floats into the bedroom.

"He's sleeping. Roland too."

A pause.

"The doctor won't say."

Another pause, longer than the first.

"We haven't had the television on, but we heard the news on the radio on the way home from the hospital. Two airplanes. Both towers."

Good thing Genevieve answered the phone.

"Terrible. They say the world will never be the same again."

Bullshit. The last thirty-six hours have taught Roland what real change is: a boy with a bandaged right eye, an eye that might always drift out of focus, unable to track the same path as the other.

Roland is perhaps six or seven years old. His oldest brother, Denis, is old enough to grow the dark outline of a beard on his jaw, but his body, thin and wiry as the tip of a willow branch, has not yet broadened into that of a man. Their father, Émile, halters the quietest horse in his string, brings the old mare in for Roland, and leaves the older brother to teach the younger how to ride.

Roland watches while Denis puts the bridle on the horse's head, persuading her to open her mouth for the bit by inserting his thumb between the soft lips and prying the teeth apart, while at the same time pulling upward on the loop of leather that goes behind the ears.

"Come here."

Roland moves closer, a bit afraid of the horse's large head.

"Put your finger in her mouth."

He hesitates. His brother makes a sound somewhere between a laugh and a snort.

"Chickenshit. If she bites, give her a good whack, right here." He points to the animal's nose. "Horses are like dogs, sensitive in the muzzle."

Roland puts his thumb into the horse's mouth, not very far, not past the barrier of her broad back teeth. The mare stands quietly.

Denis throws on the saddle and explains to him how to put his foot in the stirrup and swing himself up into the seat by grasping the pieces of leather that are used to tie a lariat below the horn. When he is taller, Roland will be able to reach the horn and swing himself up that way, the way he's seen his older brothers do it. He tries to follow the instructions, but as soon as he pulls on the leather ties, the saddle slips sideways towards him. Denis rights the saddle. Roland tries again. His older brother becomes impatient and paces the corral, finally throwing the coil of lead line and halter he's been holding into the dirt. The horse begins to shift her weight from foot to foot.

"Are you deaf? Stupid? Your left foot here, your right foot over the back."

Roland launches himself upward with his right foot, trying not to put too much weight on the ties. The saddle begins to slip, but he is able to center it on the mare by leaning over to the opposite side. It settles into place in the middle of the animal's broad back.

Denis leads the horse out of the corral and hands the boy the reins. Roland is still trying to position them between his fingers, adjusting them so each has the same amount of slack, the way he's seen his father do it, when something goes wrong. It starts with a sudden sound, unexpected and unidentifiable. The horse bolts. He clings to the reins with one hand and puts the other on the horn to keep his body from being bounced out of the saddle. The horse jumps once, twice, and each time the saddle slips further to the left. The machine shed and the granaries, newly painted, the poplar trees behind them, become a kaleidoscope of red and green. Some instinct tells him to kick his feet out of the stirrups. When he hits the ground, he loses his wind. He can't breathe. The saddle hangs upside down beneath the mare's belly, but she has moved away from him. He won't be crushed beneath her feet.

He must have cried out, because in a moment, his father is there, kneeling beside him. Roland tries to catch his breath, but each time his chest moves, he feels a pain. Émile puts a hand on the side of his son's face, and with the other checks for broken bones. When his father presses gently between his shoulder and his neck, he cries out. A fractured collarbone.

Denis stands a few feet away.

"How did this happen?" their father asks.

"He must have forgotten to check the cinch. I told him to tighten the cinch."

Roland does not know which part of the saddle is called the cinch.

"He might be too young for horses."

"I was his age when I learned," Denis said. "I didn't have any trouble."

Weeks later, when his collarbone has healed, his father gives him his second riding lesson. At the end, Émile turns the horse out with the others, slapping her lightly on the backside to encourage her to move quickly through the gate. That afternoon, Roland comes to know two things: he was never told about the cinch, which his father explains is the wide band of leather that fastens the saddle around the horse, and the sound he heard, just before the horse bolted, was the crack of his brother's palm against the old mare's flank.

Eva Lafonde gave birth to her oldest child, Denis, six months after her marriage to his father. He was conceived in the soft sand that bordered a creek bank, an act for which Émile has always blamed himself. Eva's family traced their roots back to the Dumonts, who fought for Riel in the rebellion, and as such they were expected to ignore convention. His family had no excuse. Perhaps for that reason, Émile took on the sins of his firstborn as his own. Denis was the type of kid who said fatso and four-eyes and slut, who made comments about his teachers in a voice just loud enough to be heard but not recognized. Once he turned twelve, his parents could no longer force him to go to church. Émile confessed to all of this. When Denis was seventeen years old, he left home to work the oil rigs near Leduc.

A few years later, he came back, pulled a house trailer into the farmyard and exerted his firstborn's right of place. Émile ignored the cases of empty beer bottles that piled up beside the porch step of the trailer and the cars belonging to women who spent the night. One by one, the rest of the children left the farm to make their own lives. Roy married Myra and bought his own place, just a few miles away. Joseph and Roxanna did the same. The girls went further, one even going so far as to live common-law with a Jewish lawyer in Montreal. Denis followed the rigs, away from Eyehill for months at a time, going as far as Venezuela, but between jobs, he returned to the trailer.

Roland was nineteen the year Émile's leg was crushed when a loaded hay wagon rolled backward and pinned him to the tractor wheel. The accident seemed to make an old man of him, and more and more often he left the running of the farm to his youngest son. When Eva's knees began to give out and Émile needed money to buy a house in town, a bungalow without stairs, he offered to sell the farm to Roland. Denis, being the oldest, was perhaps the more obvious choice, but he was away at the time, and even though the oil paid good wages, his money never seemed to last. Anyway, the youngest had a talent for the work, and times being what they were, there was little chance Roland would go to the seminary. The days were gone when a large family like the Lafondes could produce a priest, or at the very least a nun, thus guaranteeing themselves a hearing, if not a place, in heaven.

Roland feels as if he lived most of his life with his eyes and ears full of sand before he married Genevieve. He was ignorant of birds until she put feeders in bare branches of the crabapple tree, and the air became filled with the sound and movement of chickadees. He did not know the red of the ditch willow's bark until she showed him.

They set up house on the farm, in the same rooms that had once been full of Émile and Eva and the Lafonde children. She insisted they sleep in the smallest room upstairs, one that had been used only for storage, because, she said, she wanted him to come fresh to the bed and ready, she said, raising her fine eyebrows, to be a man and not a boy.

At the breakfast table, one day in the third February of their marriage, she tells him she will not be planting a garden in the spring. He simply nods, in a hurry to check the pen of heifers that is giving him difficulty. Fifteen of the forty have calved. He has had to pull seven of the fifteen calves, and of those seven, four were born dead. A farmer's work is a holy duty, his father told him as they drove to the lawyer to sign the papers that transferred the deed to Roland. God did not make Adam a doctor or a plumber.

Later, he walks by the garden plot as part of a circuit he travels every morning on his way back to the house. He passes Denis's empty trailer and checks the windows for frost, to make sure that the furnace has not gone out. He does this without being asked, because he feels that when Denis is gone the trailer is somehow his responsibility, like the barn and the other outbuildings in the yard.

The garden plot is a large one, a fair distance from the house and surrounded on three sides by its own windbreak of Manitoba maples. His grandmother planted the trees nearly seventy years ago. When Denis moved back home, he had put his trailer on the untreed side, maybe sixty feet away from the garden, between it and a row of wooden granaries. Snow covers the ground in thin drifts, deepest against the raspberry canes, and patches of frozen soil appear here and there. Roland thinks of the seed catalogues that come every winter, the times he has seen his wife pulling pigweed and wild portulaca, kneeling in the soft dirt, her t-shirt sleeves rolled up and tucked into her bra straps to avoid a farmer's tan like his own, her arms and legs quickly turning a rich, toffee brown in the sun. She carried water in the driest weeks, but only to the tomatoes and the flowers, so her sweet peas were always loaded with blossoms and her gladiolas stood four feet tall.

That night, pressed close to her in the dark in the narrow bed that is all the small room will hold, he asks about the garden.

"Why?"

She pulls away from him slightly and rolls onto her back. Her eyes are dark shapes, and the mobile eyebrows, the true barometer of her feelings, are impossible to read in the dark.

"No special reason."

He links his fingers with hers. "But you love the dirt." He waits, knowing from conversations in the past that silence will provide the space she needs to place her words.

"Last year, when I was on my hands and knees weeding the corn seedlings, I felt like I was being watched. I looked around, expecting to see you walking up the path behind me. But you weren't there." She pauses, and shifts a little against the sheets. "Another day, I was distracted by a flash of light, just out of the corner of my eye. I ignored it, but it came again. I looked up, to the east, to see if the sun was shining off the tractor windows or the fender of that old car you never get around to towing away."

"And . . ."

"I think Denis was watching me from the window of the trailer."

"What makes you think that?"

"As the corn grew taller, he would sometimes come out of the house and lean against the fender of the old car. Or he'd come out the back door and sit on that pile of old tires. One day, I asked him what he was doing. I remember what I said. What brings you outside in the hot sun, Denis? No harm in looking, he said."

Roland holds his body rigid on the mattress. It's natural for a horse to kick and a cat to scratch, his father used to say, but a man is different. A man has got to rise above his instincts.

When seismic testing in Eyehill led to increased drilling of ordinary wells and then to the building of a steam injection plant, Denis came home, more or less for good, and he brought Boudreau with him. They had worked together on various jobs in northern Alberta and then in Venezuela, living in a compound protected by a tall chain link fence topped by razor wire. Boudreau is older and has always been one step ahead, working as driller when Denis was just a motor man, then moving up to tool push as Denis himself advanced through the ranks to derrick hand, then driller. These days, Boudreau doesn't do rig work at all. He oversees the opening of new leases, hires the bulldozers that cut away the hillsides and level the uneven ground. His new title is consulting engineer, even though he's never been to school a day since grade eleven.

Denis and the girl are lying skin to skin on the carpet of his living room. When Boudreau first came to Eyehill, no one knew if the woman with him was his wife, his daughter or his girlfriend. She is almost twenty years younger than Boudreau and apparently just one course short of an MA in psychology. Before she met the older man at a bar in Calgary, her wealthy parents were ready to finance a counselling practice for her. That's what she told Denis.

She does not prepare for these encounters the way most women would. There is no smell of toothpaste or fresh shampoo. Boudreau is out of town at meetings in Calgary with the big boys of the oil patch. Usually, when the clothes come off, it's the women who want to talk, but Denis finds that with this girl, it's the other way around.

"Roland's wife is pregnant."

"So?"

"Why should he have so fucking much? The farm, our parent's house, a wife, a son."

"The baby could be a girl. Fifty percent chance."

"Not for Roland. He'll have a boy, and everyone will be tickled up the ass at the thought of another generation of Lafondes plowing the family soil."

She laughs. "You need to work on your issues, Denis. Find an outlet for your hostility."

"An outlet?"

"Men express themselves through what they own. Why do you think Boudreau leases the biggest pickup truck he can find? Dual wheels, long box, crew cab, four-wheel drive, monster engine. Think about it. Why does Jarvis McGowan keep buying wild horses when he never plans to break them?"

Denis pins her to the carpet with his weight. "Enough," he says. "Any more and I'll feel like I'm doing it with a textbook. Or worse, a school teacher. Doing it with a school teacher, that's Roy's department."

Boudreau's girl laughs. "Keeping things bottled up, that kind of repression has physical effects. Bad for the circulation. High blood pressure, heart attacks."

He pulls her hand down to his crotch. "Nothing wrong with my circulation."

"Other ways too. My experience is that it affects a man's timing."

Denis lets her feel the edge of his teeth against her shoulder.

"It makes everything happen just a little too quickly, if you know what I mean."

Émile taught him never to shoot another man's dog, which is why the dog tethered by Denis's trailer is still alive, muttering and growling on the end of its chain. His brother came home with the black and tan mongrel not long before Roland's son was born. It was obvious from the first day that the dog was mean.

"What good is a dog like that?" he asked Denis.

"Kills rats."

And it did, too. Tossed them in the air and snapped their spines. But it could not be taught to discriminate, killed cats the same way, and that spring began to run with the neighbour's dog. One morning, the neighbour drove through his cow herd and found a newborn calf with a torn throat. He loaded the dead animal into the back of his half-ton and brought it over to show Denis. Denis did not answer the door, so he went to Roland.

"Prices being what they are," he said, "that calf would have been worth over five hundred dollars this fall."

Roland nods.

"When I find my dog, I'm going to shoot him. You'd better tell your brother to do the same with his."

Of course, Denis refused to kill the dog, but he did start tying the animal up. It lay under the shelter of the trailer on the hottest and coldest days, and the rest of the time paced back and forth, wearing away the grass, making a large half-circle of packed dirt beside the step. It bared its teeth at anyone who passed. Roland was glad he'd plowed a new place for Genevieve's garden, closer to their own house, out of sight of the dog.

Just a few days ago, Roland would never have considered entering the trailer without Denis's permission. The door is unlocked, so he doesn't have to break a window or a hinge in order to get in the door, but it feels to him, all the same, as if something has been broken. Denis's truck left the yard early that morning. There is no evidence of the injured dog. Perhaps he took it with him. The shovel that Roland used to drive the animal away from his son leans against the porch wall.

The interior is surprisingly clean. A pile of neatly folded laundry sits on the couch. There are no grease stains beside the stove. The kitchen is tiny, but all the rooms are small, as is the way with house trailers. Not a bad place to live, Genevieve had once remarked, if you like bowling alleys. When he left the house she was trying to get their drowsy son into his clothes. They must go to the hospital again today, so the dressing can be changed and the wounds cleaned. Animal bites are notorious for infection, the doctor said, and the dog should be observed for rabies before it is put down. But now the dog is gone.

Émile always said one man should give another the benefit of the doubt.

Roland faced Denis, the bleeding boy in his arms, the dog whose ribs he had broken with the shovel lying on the ground between them.

"You let that dog off the chain."

His brother shook his head. "A kid is a goad to a dog. I didn't unsnap the chain. He pulled free. Maybe he was teased."

The dog tried to rise from the ground. Roland tensed, ready to pick up the shovel and swing it again. The boy, who had been silent with shock, began to whimper, filled his lungs with air, working up to the screams that would last all the way to the hospital, until the nurse stuck the needle in his hip.

Roland crosses the short distance from the front door of the trailer to the kitchen stove. He turns the knobs that control the heat for the burners to the highest setting. Before long, all four begin to glow red. Roland searches the bottom cupboards and comes up with a small cooking pot, thin-bottomed and made of cheap aluminum. He has half a pound of butter, stolen from Genevieve's pantry. He removes the foil, places the butter in the pot and sets the pan on one of the hot burners. Then he turns his back on it all, closes the door on the smell of scorch, and goes to help his wife with the last of their son's buttons.

"I called the municipal office as soon as I saw the smoke," Jake says, "but I bet the trailer was gone before the fire truck filled its tank."

Roland's neighbours, gathered for morning coffee at the Eyehill Café.

"I knew it was too late before I even pulled in the yard."

The men sit for a moment, thinking of the column of black smoke rising from the Lafonde farm. The Lafondes have always been unlucky. Look at Émile and the hay wagon. Joseph's wife dead of cancer before her thirty-fifth birthday. Roland's boy. The fire.

Jerry Daniels says, "Funny thing the trailer should burn so soon after Denis's dog bit the boy. It makes you wonder."

The others at the table look into their mugs or shrug their shoulders. Daniels is a drinking buddy of Denis's and, worse than that, is rumoured to have a thing for young girls. They might believe such a thing of Joseph, who is quick-tempered and hates to lose at cards, but not of Roland, who has always been one of the civilized Lafondes.

"Old trailers are known for bad wiring," Quinn says. "They need regular maintenance. A lot of care."

The rest nod their agreement; Denis is not a careful man. The waitress comes by with the coffee pot. Spoons clink against cups in a wordless choosing of sides.

Suzy Saretsky

Suzy tells everyone who asks, and there haven't been many, to call her Suzanne. She wishes the job provided her with a uniform, but it doesn't, so she has created one of her own: beige twill pants, a white t-shirt, size XL, left untucked, white running shoes, white socks. She needs the XL because of her breasts. The pants are a respectable size twelve. White looks clean and professional. The job, taken on at first as part of her disguise, has become her *raison d'être*. Back when she was a teenager attending Airedale High School, she couldn't comprehend a word of the French carefully copied on the blackboard by Mlle Beausoleil (pronounced Bozo-lay, because, the boys snickered, only a clown would sleep with her). Here, she has already learned two words, and learned them while sweeping pencil shavings from beneath the sharpener in the English classroom, no less. There, a very pregnant Mrs. Henderson-McCoy had written and underlined in heavy chalk, as an example for her students: *Children are my raison d'être — reason to be.*

Suzy slides back and forth on the patch of ice that formed overnight on the concrete pad in front of the exit near the industrial arts area, enjoying the way her body wobbles and steadies as she gains her balance. She is supposed to be scattering salt on the ice. Alvorsen, the head custodian, generally does the job because it gives him a chance to have a quick smoke with the industrial arts teacher, but he left work early this morning after having a fight with the principal.

"I won't clean up their shit," said Alvorsen.

"We try to set an example in this building, Mr. Alvorsen," the principal said. "Please lower your voice."

"You think a dirty little prick who deliberately shits in a urinal is going to be bothered by the word shit?"

Before the other man could answer, Alvorsen had grabbed his coat and hat and walked out of the building. The old man can get away with things like that because the heating system in the school is antiquated and complex, and he is the only person who knows how to keep it running. His job will be waiting for him tomorrow.

"Miss Saretsky?"

The principal has discovered her mid-slide, a bag of unused salt in her hand. She quickly grabs a handful to scatter on the ice. Some of it bounces across the shiny toes of the principal's shoes.

"Miss Saretsky, I have decided to entrust you with the fire inspection. The inspector is due to arrive within the hour. Do you remember the discussion we had earlier this morning?"

She nods.

"One more time, what is it that we strive for here at Southfield High?"

"The safety of the physical plant is our primary concern."

The winter before, when she was in grade seven, the girl had floated, hung suspended for a split, split second in midair before landing the double lutz, her blade biting into the surface of the ice, the edge holding, momentum propelling her along in a single graceful exit curve. There wasn't another girl, even among the older members of the senior classes, who could

match her. The coach said, Keep this up and next year I won't
be able to teach you a thing.

She has been skating for two months now, long enough
to understand, as she lies flat on her belly where she has fallen,
that something has gone wrong, wrong forever, and there's no
fixing it. The Eyehill Arena has become, like the Eyehill School,
a place of bitter, useless struggle, worse perhaps because her
mother, who quietly comes to her room to read aloud to her in
secret, cannot do a double lutz and pass it off as Suzy's. It is
connected to the heavy breasts that are now pressing themselves
against the ice, swollen and itchy and growing with frightening
speed, distorting the smooth torso that used to align itself so
perfectly with her hips when she rotated in the air. It is past
suppertime, and the parents of the other students have taken
them home. Her father insists on this extra hour of practice,
these extra falls. My daughter, he says, is damn well going to
make something of herself.

"You okay?"

It's the caretaker, the man who floods the ice with a fas-
cinating contraption made of a water barrel punched with holes
and a piece of carpet six feet wide to catch and spread the
leaking. He is the only other person in the building. When he
floods, all the skate marks, the weak scrapes of the beginners
and the deep gouges where a toe pick sent chips flying, all these
alike are smoothed away. Skaters learn to tighten their laces in a
hurry, hoping to be the first to make a mark on the freshly
flooded surface. His name is Jerry Daniels.

"Time for me to go to work."

She pushes herself up. He has been filling the water barrel
but stops his work to hold the door open for her. She is too shy
to say thank you, not being in the habit of speaking to him. He
follows her. She doesn't remove her skates, because there is still
over half an hour left before her father comes, but she cleans
the blades for something to do. The floor of the waiting area is

concrete, criss-crossed with paths made of thick, wide boards laid end to end. These are for the skaters, so they don't grind the edges off their blades on the gritty floor. Jerry is rearranging some of them at the far end, making a path to the padlocked door across from the bathrooms. He takes a key out of his pocket and twists open the lock with one easy movement. He picks up a short length of board and drops it inside the room. Again, he holds a door open for her.

"Want to see inside?"

She doesn't, really, but she can't think of any reason to refuse, so she walks her skater's pick-toed walk along the path of boards. Two hockey nets are piled in the corner closest to the door. The plywood archway through which the figure skaters enter and exit in each year's winter carnival leans against one wall.

"Step in," he says, and when she does, he follows, closing the door behind them.

She is trapped, stranded on the little piece of board, unable to move beyond it because the concrete floor will ruin the blades of her expensive skates. He moves very close, still behind her, breathing in her ear.

"Let me touch them."

His hand comes around to support her right breast. It doesn't hurt. The other hand moves under her left. For the first time since last summer, her chest feels weightless. Even when he squeezes a little bit, it doesn't hurt. The skin surrounding each breast seems to tighten, feels like a shiver. He leans into her, and her toe picks tip forward, digging into the wood.

"Nice," he says. "You go on now. I'll be out in a minute."

He steps aside so she can leave. He closes the door behind her, and for a few minutes she is alone in the waiting room. Then she goes back out, her skates heavy on her feet as she crosses the blue line. A door bangs, but she doesn't look toward the sound.

"Time for me to flood," Jerry says, exactly as he usually

does, the words a signal for all skaters to leave the ice. From inside, she watches him drag the barrel in ever-decreasing concentric circles. It is a cold day, and by the time he makes his last pass, the first ones have frozen. She sits down to unlace her skates just as he comes in.

"Wait," he says. "Take a few turns around the rink before you go. Next week too, if you want."

"What about the hockey players?"

At seven o'clock, the teenage boys will come to practice. The figure skaters have already had their turn, their fresh ice. That's the way it works.

"What about them?" he says.

Every stroke of her blades, left, right, left, echoes in the empty rink. She doesn't bother with the jumps, just makes her own pattern of half-circles and edges, letting herself glide backwards from time to time so she can see the tracks her skates have made. She thinks of the hockey players, the two or three who have started calling her Suzy Big-tits No-brain, rushing onto the ice and stopping, confused by the unexpected marks. Suzy Saretsky has been there before them. She can't believe how easily this came her way.

The boy in the scuffed leather jacket, cuffs rolled up, two sizes too big for his skinny body, reminds Suzy of her firstborn, Timmy. He swaggers and swears, looks at her as she pushes past with her cart of brooms as if she were the dirt that needs sweeping up. He could well be the one who shit in the urinal. Timmy's father was one of the few men she's slept with — and there have been many — whom she truly counts as a mistake.

Little Paulina, now (named after another illegitimate child, Matt Cory's daughter on *Another World*, Suzy's favourite soap before they took it off the air), she's as gentle as a lamb, just like her father, who used to drive the bread truck into Eyehill on Tuesday and Friday mornings. Paulina had been conceived

during a time when his wife had been addicted to video gambling. Suzy got to know him because he was a customer at the
Eyehill Café, where she worked on and off as a waitress. He'd
always asked for his coffee perked, with an extra teaspoon of
powdered instant added, no sugar and no cream. I like it bitter,
he'd said. A cup of this and the rest of the day is sweet. He was
a long-nosed, rather buck-toothed man who still loved his wife,
even though her gambling gave him no rest.

"I moved into the spare room. Want to know why?"

"Why?"

"So I can hide my wallet. Guess where I keep it."

"Under your pillow?"

He shakes his head.

"In my shorts. It's so bad, I have to sleep with my wallet in
my shorts."

The longer she looked at his sad face, the more his nose and
teeth receded, until he seemed quite handsome. In the end,
she did what she could to make him feel better, and felt better
herself for having done so.

Suzy knows this: go with a man into the back seat of a car
or an empty bedroom at a party. In five minutes, it's all over
and he is happy. Time after time, she marvels at how easy it is,
how different from all the hours she spent listening to her
mother read aloud in whispers from the pages of books that
grew thicker each year. Sleeping with men turned out to be
so much easier than reading what they'd written. When the
English teacher, Mr. Leeson, placed his test on her desk, anything she knew was pounded from her brain by the beating
of her heart. In the blank spaces of the test, she wrote Shake-
speare, Steinbeck, Milton, Mordecai, the names all that were
left. Single words and very small groups of words are her
strength. She's always been good with names, and if anyone is
ever stuck for the name of someone on television or a singer on
the radio, Suzy is the one to ask. She used to read the ball caps
of the men who came into the Eyehill Café: Pioneer Grain,

Ivomec, Toronto Maple Leafs, Heartland Livestock. In grade two, she won the flash card competition: hospital, mitten, many, poodle, apple, mischievous. Mrs. Erickson gave her a red ribbon. In grade four, Mrs. Lisgaard slammed her hand down on Suzy's desk with such force that the words jumped off the paper like startled frogs into a pond, and the printed page rippled like water. You aren't trying hard enough, she said. I know you know these words.

She watches the boy in the leather jacket approach a plain girl who is getting books out of her locker. He lays a heavy arm across the girl's shoulders and whispers something in her ear, laughing as her face turns red. Suzy would like to warn the girl about guys like Timmy's father. The boy has moved on down the hallway, and as another girl passes by he sticks out a foot and pretends to trip her. She stumbles a little, but she looks like an athletic girl, and she doesn't fall, just turns around and smiles, acknowledging the attention that he's paid her.

The child she misses the most is her baby, Gil (named after her favourite country singer, whose voice is as soothing as a cool bath in the midst of fever). Next month is his first birthday. When she was pregnant with him, her parents, who'd been in their forties when they'd had their one and only child, sold the farm and retired to Kelowna. The brooms in the cart remind her of her mother, a thin, tanned woman with coarse grey hair. She considers which one to use for this particular stretch of hall and thinks of her mother sweeping the kitchen floor, the crumbs she picked up and scattered for the birds to eat in wintertime. You take after me, she used to say. You have a soft heart. Her mother would have stayed behind to help with the children, if there had been any way she could possibly have done so and kept it secret from her husband.

It started the day that Suzy said, just for something to say, that she'd like to see the West Coast. The rain forest and the killer whales, the trees so big your arms wouldn't meet around the trunks. She'd like to see in real life what she sees on the Discovery Channel.

"What makes you think that it's up to you to stay here and look after these kids?"

She and Boudreau's girl are sitting at the table nearest the door of the Eyehill Café, baby Gil resting, quietly for once, in the stroller beside her chair.

"They're mine," she says, feeling stupid, knowing the answer is too short and too simple for Boudreau's girl, who was raised in Calgary, who left university just one class short of her MA in psychology, and who only wound up in Eyehill because she follows Boudreau from oilfield to oilfield.

"Don't they have fathers?"

You never know, Suzy will tell people, years later. You never know when a simple question is going to change your life.

"I'll help you arrange it," Boudreau's girl said. "I've got friends in every city in Alberta."

"Aren't there laws?"

"Depends on how badly they want to catch you. Myra Lafonde isn't going to make any trouble. Neither will the Dobsons; Paulina spends most of her time at their place already. And as for Timmy's father" — she fiddles with her lighter for a second, trying to get some fire to light her cigarette — "you're sure he *is* the father?"

"Yes."

"Well then, a paternity test will make him live up to his responsibilities." Boudreau's girl sucks deeply on her cigarette, leans back and blows the smoke out slowly, a faraway look on her face. "I'd like to be there when he takes delivery of a nearly full-grown son who has been picked up twice already for shoplifting." She jerks her chin a little to the right, indicating his wife, who is sitting at a table across the room: her expensive haircut, her pants from the same dye lot as her sweater, her position as the wife of a farmer who owns the biggest tractor in the municipality and whose land is deeded in both their names. "I'd like to be a fly on the wall," she says.

"I don't know."

"It will be good for all concerned," she says. "We psychologists call it reality therapy."

Just at that moment, when Suzy's doubts are the loudest thing in her mind, Myra Lafonde comes into the café. When she looks at baby Gil, her face lights up.

"How's our little Gilly-fish today? What are you feeding him, Suzy? He's grown three inches since last week."

Gil starts to vibrate in his stroller, kicking his legs and giggling as Myra makes big eyes at him. When each of the children was born, Myra gave them a sweater knitted from heavy wool in bright colours, with a toque to match. She gives this gift to every child born in Eyehill, and when asked how many she has made, she says she doesn't keep track. Boudreau's girl says that's bullshit, that you can tell by looking at her the woman can't help counting every child she doesn't have. Myra treats Suzy's children the same as she does her Lafonde nieces and nephews, and looked at them, when they were newborn, the way she looked at all babies, with a mixture of tenderness and regret. Her husband, Roy, is one of the few sad men in town that has not sought Suzy out.

Myra rests her hand briefly on the top of Gil's head, feeling the softness of his baby hair, then she moves on, not towards the table where the other women are sitting, but to another, where she sits by herself.

"Roy Lafonde is not Gil's father," Suzy whispers.

"Doesn't matter. We're living in the twenty-first century."

Suzy opens her mouth.

"Nowadays they make kids in tubes, for Christ's sake, and never even blink an eye. I've got a friend who sleeps with a lawyer in Calgary. She'll be able to help us with the paperwork."

Boudreau's girl puts her finger in the path of the smoke that rises from where the cigarette rests in the ashtray, watching the way it curls, then splits, then carries on as if the finger had never been there. She rolls her eyes in the direction of Myra Lafonde.

"Could be a sign from God," she says, "if there were such a thing."

She can tell right away that the fire inspector has a heavy heart. Pouches of skin sag over his eyes, his shoulders slope toward the ground, and his pants droop at the crotch and knee. He tries to hide all this with suspenders, a flash of white false teeth and an officious way of making pen marks on his clipboard.

"That pile of magazines over there," he says, tipping his pen toward the back issues that have been piling up behind the librarian's counter. "They have to be moved. Could impede a quick exit."

He makes a note.

She takes him to the art room, where he goes directly to the small room at the back that holds the kiln. The teacher, a young, nervous man who wears a black turtleneck and a black leather suit jacket, tries not to be distracted by the presence of the inspector. He continues with his lesson.

"The secret to drawing the human body is proportion. We are, all of us, six head lengths long."

The students look sceptical.

"You don't believe me?" He points a shaky finger at a boy in the front. "Come up here and measure."

The boy hesitates.

The teacher extends a twelve-inch ruler towards him. "Start with my head," he says.

"This kiln room is supposed to be locked at all times," the fire inspector roars from the back of the room.

The interruption brings startled giggles from a few students. The boy relaxes a little as the ruler is lowered.

"What?"

"That kiln has the potential to reach temperatures of two

thousand degrees. Do you know what would happen if a student wandered into that room and opened it while it was heating?"

The young man stares.

"I'll tell you what would happen. Explosion. Pieces of clay with razor-sharp edges. Severed arteries. Understand?"

Another giggle.

The inspector hikes up his pants and strides forward to survey the group of students. "You think that's funny?"

Silence.

The inspector makes a note and nods to indicate to Suzy that they can move on. The noise level in the room rises as soon as his back is turned. She sees one of the students eyeing the door of the kiln room, wondering. She hears the teacher say, "The ancient Romans —" before the door swings shut.

On their way to the furnace room, they must pass the gym, one of the few spaces in the school that does not require inspection because it is four walls of painted cinderblock and not much else. Nonetheless, the inspector stops. He looks through the window. The boys inside are playing basketball, the outline of their shoulder blades visible beneath the loose jerseys, their legs long and bony, propelling them into the air. The inspector lifts his hand to his face, placing his thumb next to the inner corner of one eye. He drops his head and looks at the floor, as if the sight of running boys is more than he can bear.

She knew it. A heavy heart.

The furnace room is shadowy; one of the light bulbs burned out and Alvorsen hasn't replaced it. The inspector follows her in and shuts the door. The machinery, old and noisy, hums and thumps, the compressors pounding out a sound that reminds Suzy of waking up in the middle of the night alone with your heartbeat. The difference is that the furnace room is soothing. Babies would be lulled asleep here, the way they are in the back seats of moving cars.

"What's wrong?" she asks.

"I have a son. Twenty-one years old."

The furnace kicks in. The skinny little chemistry teacher has nudged up her thermostat again.

"He's not right. Not right in the head."

She hesitates. She and Boudreau's girl had an agreement. I'll give up cigarettes, the other girl said, if you give up sleeping with men who look like they've been kicked in the balls.

"He wasn't born that way. He was in grade three when it happened. Came home from school feeling sick. My head aches, he said. My old mother was living with us then, and she was always complaining about something, a pain in her chest or her neck or her stomach. I thought he was picking up the habit from her."

She moves so she is leaning against the wall beside him, her shoulder touching his arm.

"Kids your age don't get headaches. That's what I told him."

He looks at the maze of pipes overhead.

"When I think of what happened, I think the meningitis moved like a fire through his brain. When I walk through a building like this one, I think of every room as part of what he was."

She can't help it. She slides her hand over his leg, downward to the knee, then up again. The progress of her fingers is stopped when he brings the clipboard down and rests the edge of it against his thigh, creating a barrier.

"Doesn't work. I tried it once, years ago. Doesn't make a difference."

He straightens his body away from hers and focuses his attention on the gigantic fuse box to the left of the door. He flips open the clipboard and flicks the pen along the page.

"He gets excited when I pull into the driveway. My wife says he knows the sound of my truck."

Suzy watches him mark his charts, her hand in her pocket, fingers pressing on the sharp edges of keys. Before she gave up

going to parent-teacher interviews, she'd been told repeatedly
that Timothy was a bright boy, that he could do much, much
better. She used to pass this qualified praise on to her son, until
she figured out that he was the type who would do exactly the
opposite of what he guessed would please adults. By the time
she caught on, he was too old, and it was too late to say, Timmy, I wish that once, just once, you would break your mother's
heart.

The end of the inspection coincides with the beginning of her
coffee break. She leaves the fire inspector at the door to the
principal's office and hurries to the cluttered broom closet that
is the custodians' staff room. Alvorsen is gone for the day, and
Bitsy, the woman who works the later shift, won't arrive until
the dismissal bell, so Suzy has the room to herself. Each of them
has an allotted space, perhaps twice the size of a shoebox, for
the storage of personal items. Bitsy the Organized created the
system, her small hand extended, her small finger pointing,
her little size-five feet planted squarely to withstand opposi-
tion. Your stuff over there, she told Alvorsen, and the old man
meekly moved the more-than-one-hundred tiny parts of the
model ship, the little hooded reading lamp whose light was
crucial to the assembly of those parts, and the tube of glue.
The noxious fumes bother his wife, which is why he pursues
his hobby while at work rather than in his leisure time. Bitsy's
space houses a clean coffee cup and an assortment of Tupper-
ware containing various powders and bits of dried leaves, which
she mixes, a little of this, a little of that, according to the barometer on the wall immediately above them. Air pressure gives
my arthritis fits, she says, boiling the electric kettle which
belongs to her but which she shares with them. She used to take
a pill that gnawed at her guts like a rat in a grain bin, but now
she believes that herbs are the thing. Her weekly read, *Soap
Opera Digest*, takes all the space that remains. Suzy's spot is

nearly empty: a bag of jelly beans, a box of pencils, erasers, and a ruler, things she collects when she sweeps the floor, and a quilted case for cosmetics because she likes to keep her eyeliner fresh.

Her heart is beating very fast. Her palms are damp, and she feels as if there is not enough air in the room, but she has to go ahead with it. All day, as she swept the halls, cleaned the glass in the double doors, even as she had her hand on the fire inspector's leg, part of her has been preoccupied, anxious to test what she learned while sweeping up the pencil shavings in Mrs. Henderson-McCoy's classroom.

Bitsy won't mind if she borrows the magazine. She opens it at random and spreads it on the table in front of her. The words begin to move, as usual, each letter dripping into the one below, until the page resembles an anthill that's been kicked, a swarm of letters that makes her skin crawl. This is the moment when she feels she could throw up. The moment when she'd asked Mrs. Erickson, How can I keep all these dogs on one leash? Mrs. Erickson sighed and said, Suzy, this is a story about a girl who rescues her little brother from a swamp. There are no dogs in it.

The fact that Mrs. Henderson-McCoy had underlined the words on the blackboard seemed to be what made the difference. She reaches for the ruler and a green pencil crayon, because green is her lucky colour. The ruler is an old-fashioned one, made of wood, so, when she turns it over so that the numbers are not visible, it blocks her view of the moving words below, making a boundary between them and the single, first line of the paragraph above it. She closes her eyes for a minute. When she opens them, she sees that the words along the ruler's edge still stir with a gentle vibration, leaving slight ghosts of themselves behind, but they cannot jump the ruler fence. By looking very hard, she can read most of them: *next week, the wedding of Royce and Brianna.* Her fingers tremble around the pencil, but she pushes hard against the paper, making a firm, green line along the ruler. Bitsy will understand, and anyway it's Friday, and she'll have a new one on Monday. This is the part that counts. She slides the ruler carefully downward, until it rests below the second line. The words above stay in their places, contained by the pencil line. The second line continues: *is threatened by the unexpected appearance of.* This is a story. She is reading: *her twin sister, Diana.* Through the middle of it all, the wedding, the story, the small dark room, Suzy has a thought that surges, full of righteous joy. Fuck you. Fuck every single one of you.

River Judith

Quinn lies flat on his back on the crest of a hill, face to the sky, dry rustle of grass all around him. Soon the cows will come, walking up the hill, their legs black from the mud of the slough bottom. He doesn't have to deepen his voice and call out, or lure them with a pail of oats. Lie completely still and they will find you — a trick he learned as a boy. He shifts his hips, and the soft soil holds the shape of his body. Arms stretched out, he digs his fingers into the wiry grass. One fist closes on a handful of sage, and for a second the air is bittersweet with the smell of the silver leaves, bleached by sun and October frost.

Before long, he hears them, close and breathing. One leans over, her moist nose frisking him for scent of danger. A fly, made stupid by the unexpected warmth of the day, buzzes near Quinn's head. He opens his eyes. His cows look different from this angle; large-headed, long-muzzled and imposing, they form the beginning of a ring around his body. The one with her nose to him snorts and steps back, front foot just inches from his head.

Twenty years ago, his father had been right. Oil prices fell. The wells shut down. Tanks rusted. The roads tanker trucks had worn in the sandy pasture soil grew over and were criss-crossed by the winding paths of cattle on their way to drink.

Quinn wishes he'd said, Jarvis, just wait the bastards out.

"That horse lame?" Quinn asks.

"Back left foot." Jarvis helps him slip a halter on the mare. While Quinn leads her to the barn, Jarvis talks crazy to the horse, like some people do with babies, "Sweet, sweet sugar girl. Pretty little one."

Quinn bends over and picks up the mare's foot, running his hand over the fetlock, checking for swelling or wounds.

"You hear about Boudreau?" Jarvis asks.

"No."

"He bought Roy Lafonde's quarter by the creek. Boudreau's girlfriend told Carmela all about it at the coffee shop. First thing the girl's going to do when her and Boudreau move in is knock out some walls and make herself an office."

"For certain? I wouldn't think Roy'd want to sell."

"He works all winter, plowing leases. Boudreau hires and fires. Roy needs the job."

Quinn takes a hoof pick out of his back pocket.

Jarvis continues, "Now Carmela thinks she'll put the girls together in one room and take the other for herself. A sewing room, but she wants a bed in it."

The horse shifts slightly. Jarvis lays a hand on her flank to settle her. "Quiet, sweet sugar, quiet."

Quinn's never figured it out. Does the younger man's luck run high or low? Jarvis's father gave him two sections of land, the worst ground in the area, stones and sagebrush, but people said, He's lucky — never had to pay a penny for it. Carmela is another of Jarvis's mixed blessings. She's kept her hair long and her body slim, and you'd never know she's had two kids, but her laughter lingers on other men's jokes.

He uses the pick to gently probe the bottom of the foot. Talking about Carmela reminds Quinn to be grateful for his own wife. When he first met Maggie, she'd been working as a teller at the CIBC, dating a lawyer. Seven months later, he'd asked her to marry him and she said yes. He'd never expected such a gift, and from a bank, of all places.

"You know what Carmela said yesterday? What she called me?"

Quinn thinks of things she has called Jarvis in the past. Son of a bitch. Dumb fuck. Prick.

"Emotionally distant."

The horse is getting restless. Quinn presses slightly with the sharp end of the pick.

"She'll sleep in that sewing room," Jarvis says. "I know she will."

Quinn pops the stone out of the soft underside of the hoof. It's grown so dark in the barn that he can't see where it lands. Jarvis loves Carmela. There's nothing Quinn can do.

The old man is recovering from injuries he suffered when he lost the use of the right side of his body and rolled the tractor down a steep incline. A mild stroke, the doctor said. While his father sleeps, Quinn, two years into a science degree, sits by the bed with a textbook, studying for midterm exams.

Hydrology. The movement of water underground, water older than the glaciers, coming to the surface here and there. Sloughs forming in depressions. Water retreating in drought, leaving saline soils and alkali flats as evidence of where it once lay. The Judith River, subterranean and huge, sixty million years old, meltwater from the tectonic thrust that formed the Rocky Mountains. Quinn writes *aquifer* on a piece of paper so he can memorize it later.

His father moves beneath the sheets, restless, then awake. He looks in Quinn's direction.

"Wait the bastards out," he says.

Quinn, still thinking *aquifer*, doesn't understand.

"Do you need to write it fucking down or what?"

"No."

"Wait the bastards out. Somebody owns them," his father said, "some suit from the East, maybe, or they answer to a guy who dresses in white skirts like a woman and has twenty wives to make up for it. One day the crews will get a call that says leave, and they'll go."

1976. Price of crude oil is up, and seismic trucks are parked three and four at a time on Main Street. There are knocks on farmhouse doors and men nobody's ever seen before, standing on the step with briefcases and contracts.

"What do you want me to do?" Quinn asks.

"Sign. Don't Sign. Doesn't matter. We'll be here long after they're gone."

A massive hemorrhage of the brain less than forty-eight hours later. When the doctors explained it, Quinn thought of a ruptured fire hydrant, spraying twenty, thirty feet into the air, the flow uncontrollable once the valve opened. The end of his father. The start of Quinn farming. No chance to write *a water-bearing rock formation*: the definition of an aquifer.

The highest point of land for miles, and Quinn owns it. He likes to think it's the place that gave Eyehill its name. Sand shows through the steep, soft slope in places where the grass is thin. The steam injection plant sits at the foot of the hill, just a few hundred yards from his property line. He hasn't signed the papers, but diagonal drilling makes it possible for them to take oil from beneath his ground without permission. They get away with that and more.

At night, all lit up, the plant looks like a ship. Not far to the east, there is a small fire in the sky, a flare from a sour gas well. To the south, the lights of drilling rigs. There are noticeably fewer lights to the north, just a scattering from his neighbours' yards. Underneath them all, the Judith spreads itself as far south as Montana, moving imperceptibly through rock and soil. The steam is made from its water, three hundred gallons per minute, vaporized, then forced back into the earth to heat the sluggish oil.

His night vision is good. He can make out the pale shape of an animal watching the truck from a nearby poplar bluff. A mule deer or a large coyote. When he leaves the house in the middle of the night, he never has to flip a switch. Maggie doesn't know, he moves that quietly. Never lets on she knows, anyway. There are nights when the bed is too small, so he gets up and goes downstairs. The dining room closes in on him, then the kitchen. He presses the power and mute buttons simultaneously, filling the living room with silent, flickering light. There isn't space enough for him and the fish-mouthed people on the screen.

On the high top of the hill with the truck shut off, Quinn thinks about the cross fences he put in six months ago and the last two years of drought and blowing dirt. He thinks about his dead boy — premature and stillborn. In the darkness, Quinn listens to the steam plant pumping water from beneath the earth, changing it, sending it back again poisonous with salt.

The low-flying planes come first. Geologists take pictures from the air. Surveyors lay chain, marking the path for crews of men specially trained to set explosives beneath the ground. A young man with a tuft of chin whiskers knocks on Quinn's door. He drinks coffee at Quinn's table and talks about boyhood visits to an uncle's farm.

"I know what it's like to be a farmer," he says. "I know hard times."

Quinn looks at the papers the kid has spread out in front of him.

"The company pays good money for access. All you have to do is give us permission. We knock down a few trees, maybe. Easiest paycheque you'll ever cash."

"No thanks," Quinn says.

"We fix the fences we cut, you've got my word on that."

"No thanks."

"Maybe you'd like to talk to someone higher up?"

A few days later, Boudreau comes out to the shop where Quinn checks belts on the swather. Three more hot days and the barley will be ready to cut.

"The thing you might not understand about seismic work," says Boudreau, "is we got to test in a line. Can't be any gaps in the line. If we can't cross your property, we might just as well pack up the trucks and go home."

"Drive carefully, " Quinn says. "Watch for deer in the coulee."

His suit has already been hung in the closet. Quinn picks up the black dress that Maggie's mother bought her and places it beside the jacket. Outside, pockets of snow still sit in shady places, but the sun is hot, so he puts on a short-sleeved workshirt. His wife stepped out of the dress, swallowed two pills and now lies motionless beneath the covers of the bed.

Fence posts and wire. The ten-pound maul. Quinn loads them all into the truck and drives the short distance to the pasture closest to the yard. He starts the first of the cross-fences that will split the half-section into eight parcels, all too small to be practical, just a few days' grazing on each one. He lifts the maul, pounds, lifts and pounds, his gloves left on the seat of the truck. By dusk, the wooden handle of the maul has raised blisters beneath the thick calluses on his palms. He stretches the wire tight as guitar string. The blisters rupture, and the burn travels from the raw skin of his hands up his forearms to his elbows. Sweat dampens his workshirt. Every now and then, when a cool wind blows from the east, he catches the sulphur smell of sour gas from Roy Lafonde's well.

Jarvis comes just as it grows too dark to see where the wire meets the post. He takes the maul, grabs Quinn by the wrists and examines the ruined palms.

"Jesus, Quinn," he says, shaking his head, digging the first aid kit from behind the seat of the truck.

"I don't want to hear it," Quinn says.

Maggie never stirs beneath the covers. The windows are hung with blankets to keep out the sun. He sets a full glass of fresh water by the bed each morning. She must get up to use the bathroom, must do it when he is out of the house. Day after day, Quinn builds fences. At night, he comes in and eats macaroni casseroles brought over by the neighbours' wives.

When the last post is pounded, he saddles a horse and moves two hundred steers from their winter corrals to the newly divided half-section. He sorts the cattle into bunches, moving them from one enclosure to the next. One day he sorts for colour: black white-faced steers in one place, red in another, buckskins in the corner. Another day, he sorts by weight. His driven cattle and the patient horse grow thin.

One night, Maggie is sitting up when Quinn comes to bed, her hair brushed and her teeth cleaned, shoulders naked above the blue comforter. Quinn's back aches from days on horseback. What is the right thing to say? He takes her face gently in his two hands and touches his forehead to hers.

Maggie reaches between his thighs. The hand is cold.

"Doctor said we should give it some time," he says, leaning back to look at her.

"I'm thirty-six and you'll be forty-four next month."

"I'm not sure —"

The look on her face stops him. Such anger, fierce and unexpected, like the time their dog, frightened by thunder, sank its teeth into his wrist.

Quinn does what she wants, but he has to think of every dirty thing he's ever seen or heard, has to think again of his first brief time all those years ago, with Suzy Saretsky, in a dark room in the early hours of a party that she'd later left with someone else.

———————

There's an alkali patch where the slough used to be. The place needs cleaning up. Rusty wire curls half-buried in the crusted soil, the remains of a fence that stood beside the slough when Quinn was a boy. During the wet years, water levels rose. A few posts still stand, white lines marking the place where they were once submerged in water.

Maggie had coffee with Boudreau's girl this morning. When Quinn came in for dinner, his wife was unpacking groceries. She took milk and cottage cheese out of a bag. She opened the fridge door and slid pickle jars back and forth, trying to make room. With her back to him and her head in the fridge, she said, "My needs in this marriage aren't being met."

He watched her turn around, felt the cold draft from the still-open door.

"You know what the problem is, Quinn?"

He wants more time to answer than she is willing to give.

"You're emotionally distant."

Some people think alkali soil is a thing of drought, and it is, but water had to be there first, had to seep up in a slow dissolve through layers of earth in order to leave the bitterness behind. Quinn steps onto the powdery surface of the slough bed, leaning over to tug on a piece of wire.

A truck drives up. Carl Lisgaard, a neighbour who farms two sections next to Quinn's, rolls down the window.

"Got enough grass to hold you?" he asks.

"Rain'd help," Quinn says, coming over to lean against the truck door.

"Government don't give a rat's ass, so long as we starve to death one at a time and do it quietly," Carl says. "I'm selling my steers on Friday. Market's never so bad it couldn't get worse."

For a while, talk is about prices per pound and the criminal commissions charged by auctioneers. Finally, Carl says, "I got a daughter in college, you know that, Quinn?"

Quinn nods.

"A cheque from the oil company would go a long way towards expenses."

Boudreau has been a busy man.

The wind comes up not long after Carl drives away. Fine as ash, the alkali lifts from the surface of the slough bed. Quinn walks through the white toward his truck. He tries out the words. Emotion. Distance. Dust burns his throat.

Maggie wakes him in the night. "Someone's in the house."

Quinn hears a crazy tinkle of wind chimes by the door. Boots on the porch steps, then the hollow sound of something heavy dropped on the washing machine. He pulls on his pants and walks downstairs, sure-footed in the dark.

The black shape of a man bends over the white bulk of the washer.

"That you, Jarvis?"

"Yeah."

"Let me tell Maggie."

"Don't want to worry Maggie."

"I know."

Once he turns on the light, Quinn can see that Jarvis is drunk, a sombre type of inebriation, unexpected and frightening, because alcohol usually puts Jarvis in the mood to belt out songs no one has ever heard of. "The Cat's Pyjamas." "Boogie Woogie Butterfly." Tonight he stares and says nothing. Quinn takes him to the kitchen.

"Coffee? Something to eat?" Jarvis won't look at him.

"She's gone."

"Who?"

"Carmela. Staying with Boudreau and his fucked-up girl-friend."

Quinn turns on the tap to fill the coffee pot.

"She said she's been planning it for weeks. She's taking the girls with her. Got a job in Saskatoon, starts in three days. Boudreau knew all along. The son of a bitch checked well leases on my place yesterday. Drillers left them in a hell of a mess. Come over for a drink sometime, he says."

"She might change her mind."

"Son of a bitch lied through his teeth. He knew all along." Jarvis stares at the empty cup Quinn puts in front of him. "He's due to check leases on my south place tomorrow. No way. Not one foot on my property. I won't have it."

"Carmela could be back home by morning. Sleep here tonight." Quinn leads him to the couch. Jarvis lies down like an obedient child. Quinn sits in the matching armchair.

"I got my rifle in the truck."

The room seems too small.

"No one would blame you," Quinn says.

Two boys play with bikes. Feet off the pedals, they fly down a sloping street on the west side of Eyehill, slowed down only by the tufts of hardy grass that root their way along cracks in the sidewalk. At first, they don't recognize the sound that precedes the car speeding toward the railway track. The car, going very fast, ignores the stop sign at the crossing. Lights flash. The noise is a siren. At the bottom of the street, inside a small house built in 1946 for a man who lost his thumb fighting the Nazis, two mothers leave the kitchen table to go to the window. The police car speeds past. They hurry out the door, onto the step, hoping to see which way the cops are going.

The car stops on Main Street. The police enter the Eyehill Café and escort Boudreau's girl outside. She sits in the car with them. An ambulance drives right by. People looking out the café windows trying to catch a glimpse of the ambulance see her banging her head against the backseat of the police car. One of the customers, his ears damaged to the point of deafness by fifty years of diesel engine noise, reads her lips. She is saying no, no, no. Last week, she explained it all to a woman whose child had found the family dog run over on the road. Denial is the first stage.

The deaf man says to the small crowd gathered behind him, "Boudreau's been shot. Jarvis shot Boudreau."

Quinn is on his way to check the pump that moves water from the dugout to the trough where one of his herds goes to drink. On his way home, he'll stop by Jarvis's place. Too early to go yet. He doesn't want Jarvis to think he's checking up on him. The truck slows as it takes the hill. He puts a little more pressure on the gas pedal. When he reaches the top, he can see a long ribbon of dust, marking the way to town.

Every time he gets this close to Eyehill, Quinn automatically looks toward the spot where the grain elevator used to stand. The Wheat Pool demolished it last spring, first week of May, hot as midsummer and already dry. Everyone, even Skipper Jake, had gathered on Main Street to watch the building collapse. The year before, Joseph Lafonde had driven down Main Street on his way home from the hospital where his wife lay jaundiced and dying. He'd seen Jake on the top of the elevator, looking like he was going to jump, and he'd pulled his truck up, taken a fence post from the back, and begun pounding it against the building's metal siding. You've got no fucking right, Joseph yelled between blows, no fucking right. After school, children on their way to the skating rink ran their hands over the dents the post had made and told each other the story.

When it was over, the elevator down in a thirty-second tumble of lumber and dust, some of the men went to the beer parlour and drank until midnight, when the owner made the last of them go home. Jarvis, Quinn and the Lafonde brothers, some steadier on their feet than others, walked out into the night with a case of off-sale. They leaned against Jarvis's truck and faced east, looking at the strip of gravel road that led across the tracks to where the elevator had fallen. He can play that night in his mind like pressing rewind on the VCR.

"Seventy years," Jarvis says, raising his bottle slightly to salute the empty space. "My people hauled wheat up that road nearly seventy years."

One of the Lafonde brothers throws his bottle in a high arc toward the strip of sky that used to be blocked by the elevator's bulk.

"Time to go home," Quinn says.

Everyone agrees, but no one moves. The men stay where they are, drunk and hollow because they've eaten nothing since dinner, watching the rise of an unseasonable harvest moon, its light made red by the dust of their grandfathers' grain.